Lynch Mob!

"There's a crowd in front of the saloon just begging to become a lynch mob," Clint told Masterson. "We've got to keep them from seeing Lenny."

Suddenly there was the sound of shouting, and Clint and Bat quickly moved around the corner to see what was happening.

The mob from the saloon had obviously spotted Lenny and people were running toward him. Poor Lenny was rooted to where he stood, not knowing what the hell was going on.

"Jesus," Bat said, "they'll tear him to pieces!"

Clint and Bat broke into a run, but it was clear that the mob was going to reach Lenny before they did. They did the only thing they could do to save the kid.

They drew their guns. . . .

Also in THE GUNSMITH series

MACKLIN'S WOMEN
THE CHINESE GUNMAN
BULLETS AND BALLOTS
THE RIVERBOAT GANG
KILLER GRIZZLY
NORTH OF THE BORDER
EAGLE'S GAP
CHINATOWN HELL
THE PANHANDLE SEARCH
WILDCAT ROUNDUP
THE PONDEROSA WAR
TROUBLE RIDES A FAST HORSE
DYNAMITE JUSTICE
THE POSSE
NIGHT OF THE GILA
THE BOUNTY WOMEN
WILD BILL'S GHOST
THE MINER'S SHOWDOWN
ARCHER'S REVENGE
SHOWDOWN IN RATON
WHEN LEGENDS MEET
DESERT HELL
THE DIAMOND GUN
DENVER DUO
HELL ON WHEELS
THE LEGEND MAKER
WALKING DEAD MAN
CROSSFIRE MOUNTAIN
THE DEADLY HEALER
THE TRAIL DRIVE WAR
GERONIMO'S TRAIL
THE COMSTOCK GOLD FRAUD
BOOMTOWN KILLER
TEXAS TRACKDOWN
THE FAST DRAW LEAGUE
SHOWDOWN IN RIO MALO
OUTLAW TRAIL
HOMESTEADER GUNS
FIVE CARD DEATH
TRAILDRIVE TO MONTANA
TRIAL BY FIRE
THE OLD WHISTLER GANG
DAUGHTER OF GOLD
APACHE GOLD

PLAINS MURDER
DEADLY MEMORIES
THE NEVADA TIMBER WAR
NEW MEXICO SHOWDOWN
BARBED WIRE AND BULLETS
DEATH EXPRESS
WHEN LEGENDS DIE
SIXGUN JUSTICE
MUSTANG HUNTERS
TEXAS RANSOM
VENGEANCE TOWN
WINNER TAKE ALL
MESSAGE FROM A DEAD MAN
RIDE FOR VENGEANCE
THE TAKERSVILLE SHOOT
BLOOD ON THE LAND
SIXGUN SHOWDOWN
MISSISSIPPI MASSACRE
THE ARIZONA TRIANGLE
BROTHERS OF THE GUN
THE STAGECOACH THIEVES
JUDGMENT AT FIRECREEK
DEAD MAN'S JURY
HANDS OF THE STRANGLER
NEVADA DEATH TRAP
WAGON TRAIN TO HELL
RIDE FOR REVENGE
DEAD RINGER
TRAIL OF THE ASSASSIN
SHOOT-OUT AT CROSSFORK
BUCKSKIN'S TRAIL
HELLDORADO
THE HANGING JUDGE
THE BOUNTY HUNTER
TOMBSTONE AT LITTLE HORN
KILLER'S RACE
WYOMING RANGE WAR
GRAND CANYON GOLD
GUNS DON'T ARGUE
GUNDOWN
FRONTIER JUSTICE
GAME OF DEATH
THE OREGON STRANGLER

THE Gunsmith

116

THE OREGON STRANGLER

J. R. ROBERTS

JOVE BOOKS, NEW YORK

THE OREGON STRANGLER

A Jove Book/published by arrangement with
the author

PRINTING HISTORY
Jove edition/August 1991

ISBN: 0-515-10651-8

Jove Books are published by The Berkley Publishing Group,
200 Madison Avenue, New York, New York 10016.
The name "JOVE" and the "J" logo
are trademarks belonging to Jove Publications, Inc.

PRINTED IN THE UNITED STATES OF AMERICA

10 9 8 7 6 5 4 3 2 1

PROLOGUE

Bat Masterson watched the Oregon Strangler at work.

The Strangler's real name was Lenny Younger, and Bat had "discovered" him in Virginia. The boy was six foot eight and weighed well over three hundred pounds. He'd been working on a farm with his mother, but Bat had seen the boy's potential. Younger was twenty years old, and he wasn't that smart, but with his size and a little instruction, Bat had thought he could turn him into a successful wrestler.

They'd started in Virginia, wrestling at county fairs, but too many people knew who Lenny was. It was hard to be six foot eight and remain unknown. Bat decided to take Younger and leave Virginia, leave the South. Younger had been concerned about his mother, but Bat had assured him that they would be sending money home to her.

When Bat decided to leave the South with Lenny Younger, though, he hadn't expected to go as far north as Oregon.

They'd traveled west first, working their way to California, making enough to send to Younger's mother some decent money. From Los Angeles they worked their way north through San Jose, San Francisco, and Sacramento. Pickings were not so good in California, though. In the larger cities they were more interested in boxing. Bat thought that the kid might make a decent boxer, but he wasn't through with his wrestling scam yet.

They went from California to Oregon, and there they struck gold.

The man who was preparing to face Lenny Younger was a big man, almost as tall as Lenny and *maybe* heavier.

As of the past few weeks, Lenny had begun to wear a mask and was being called the "Oregon Strangler" by Bat Masterson. Bat thought the name might give Lenny a psychological edge. Some men who might have wrestled him did not because of the name, but there were enough men willing to try that the wrestling thing was still a moneymaker. When it ceased being a moneymaker, Bat would give Lenny his cut and send him back to the farm in Virginia.

For now, it was still working like a charm.

Bat watched the challenger remove his shirt, revealing a rock-hard chest and bulging biceps.

"This is a big one, kid," Bat said. He couldn't see Lenny's face because of the mask, but the kid nodded. The mask had cutouts for the eyes and mouth and a small one at the nose so Lenny could breathe. Other than that, Lenny was unrecognizable.

Although the challenger looked formidable enough, Bat felt sure that Lenny would be able to triumph. He didn't think that the challenger had Lenny's stamina, which he had found to be almost limitless.

"All right," the challenger said. "I'm ready."

He was surrounded by his friends and well-wishers, people who had seen Lenny run through many a challenger over the past week at this particular fair. They were hoping—and betting—that this time the challenger was good enough.

Bat made more money in side bets than he did from the

people running the fairs. That had been his plan all along.

"All right," Bat called out to the people. "Let's have the combatants in the ring."

The "ring," such as it was, was a circle drawn upon the ground. If and when the wrestlers went beyond the circle, they would have to break and come back into the ring before they hooked up again.

Lenny Younger, the Oregon Strangler, stepped into the circle. He was wearing a tight-fitting outfit that looked almost like long underwear. Bat didn't allow him to go bare-chested, because he had a scar that would make him easy to identify.

"The challenger," Bat said.

The other man stepped into the circle, and now only Bat separated the two men.

"All right then," Bat said, holding his hands out so that each palm was resting against a man's chest. He hesitated, then abruptly dropped his hands, backed away, and called out, "Wrestle."

The two men came together like two bulls.

ONE

Clint Adams had traveled north from Sacramento because he'd heard from a fellow traveler that Oregon was fertile ground for a gunsmith. He had only to stop at the first town he came to to find out that was true.

Now, a week after entering Oregon, never having spent more than one day in any town but finding work everywhere he went, he entered the town of Placerville.

Placerville looked like most of the Oregon towns he had been to so far. Ramshackle wooden structures, wet, hard ground, boardwalks in need of repair. The only thing that separated this town from the others was the fact that a traveling fair had been set up north of it. Clint, having ridden in from the south, had not seen the fair, but he'd make a point of it while he was here. It was a long time since he had been to a circus or fair.

He went first to the livery, driving his rig down the sodden, puddle-infested main street. He pulled his coat tightly around him, raising the collar to cut down on the draft that was hitting the back of his neck.

"Gunsmith, are you?" the liveryman asked.

Clint studied the man's face for some sign that he had recognized him, then decided that the man was simply asking if he were *a* gunsmith, not *the* Gunsmith.

"That's right."

"Well, plenty of work for you hereabouts."

"That's what I heard," Clint said. "Mind if I set up shop in your livery?"

"Well . . ." the man said, rubbing his jaw.

"I'll pay you ten percent of whatever I make." It was the same deal he had made in all the other towns.

To a man, he'd found the liverymen to be fair, and this one was no different. He nodded and said, "Sounds fair. Go on and set up near the back."

"You'll care for my stock?"

"Sure will, especially that big black gelding you got there. I ain't seen an animal that big and powerful in years."

"Take good care of him then."

"Oh, I will."

"I've got some fliers. Would anyone mind if I posted them around town?"

"I doubt it, but you kin ask. Lots of people will be at the fair though."

"I figured that. Is there a good restaurant in town?"

"There's two. One is the hotel, and the other is Louisa's cafe, a block beyond the hotel."

"Which has better food?"

"Both are pretty good."

"Which has better coffee?"

The man smiled, revealing more than one gap in his teeth. "That'd be Louisa, for sure."

"Thanks. Would you walk my rig back and unhitch the team? I'll be back later."

"Sure thing, mister. You any good?"

"Sorry?"

"As a gunsmith," the man said. "You any good? We gonna make some money?"

Clint smiled now and said, "Mr. . . ."

"Call me Joshua."

"Well, Joshua, we're going to make a ton of money."

Joshua smiled and said, "That's the kinda talk I like to hear."

Before posting his fliers, Clint went to the hotel to get a room. He wanted a hot bath, but he'd do that after he put up the fliers and had a drink. Following the bath he'd go looking for some food. After that, he might check out the fair.

He left most of his gear in the room and went around to post the fliers. Most of the storekeepers he requested permission from granted it, and he tacked up his first poster right next to another one that caught his eye right away.

It read: "Bat Masterson Presents His Undefeated Wrestler, THE OREGON STRANGLER. ONE HUNDRED DOLLARS to Any Man Who Can Go Three Rounds with the STRANGLER. FIVE HUNDRED to Anyone Who Can Defeat Him."

"Sonofabitch," Clint said aloud, and then he tipped his hat and excused himself to some ladies who were passing at that moment.

Clint hadn't seen Bat in some time. It would be good to see him. It wasn't surprising to him that Bat had some kind of scam going. He was interested in seeing this Oregon Strangler at work.

He finished posting his fliers and then went to the saloon. He saw the cafe right across the street and meant to stop there after one beer.

"What'll it be?" the bartender asked.

"Beer," Clint said. "Cold."

The bartender grinned and said, "Mister, cold is something we got plenty of up here."

Clint hunched his shoulders and said, "I've noticed."

The bartender brought the beer, and it was indeed ice-cold.

"Not doing much business today, are you?" Clint asked the bartender.

"Won't do much until tonight. Days, most people are at the fair."

"I heard about that. I heard they have a wrestler there who's pretty good."

"The Oregon Strangler," the bartender said. "He can't be beat. I know—I tried and a lot of my friends have tried."

Clint looked at the bartender. He was a strapping man in his midthirties, probably six-two and certainly more than two hundred pounds.

"Were your friends as big as you?"

"Some bigger," the bartender said, "but none of us were able to last three rounds, let alone beat the man."

"What's so great about him?"

"Well, he's big. Jesus, he must be six foot eight at least, but that's not the biggest thing about him."

Clint found that funny. "Six-eight? What's the biggest thing?"

"He doesn't get tired."

"He doesn't tire?"

"He doesn't *seem* to."

"Sounds interesting."

"You can see for yourself. They should be ready to take on more comers in a couple of hours."

"How many times a day does he wrestle?"

"It depends on how many challengers there are. I think the kid could go on all day."

"Kid?"

The bartender shrugged. "Maybe he's not a kid. I just get that impression."

"Well, maybe I'll take a look," Clint said. He finished the beer, put down the mug, dropped a coin on the bar, and said, "Thanks for the drink."

"Any time. I can use the company."

"How much longer will the fair be here?"

The man shrugged again. "As long as it's making money, I guess."

"That figures," Clint said. He himself might be in Placerville that long as well. "Thanks again."

He left the saloon and started across the street. He decided to bypass the bath and go straight to the cafe.

He was famished.

TWO

As Joshua the liveryman had indicated, the coffee at Louisa's was excellent. It was hot, black, and strong, the way Clint liked his coffee.

Louisa was a surprise. She was just the way Clint liked his women. She was mature—in her thirties—and full-bodied. She had a handsome face that became pretty when she smiled—and she smiled a lot.

There was nothing flirtatious between them. When he walked in the place was empty, except for one other customer. A woman approached him, wiping her hands on the apron she wore around her waist.

He suddenly wished he'd gone back to the hotel to take a bath first.

"Can I help you?"

"I was told that the food was good here and the coffee better. Is that true?"

"You've been talking to Joshua."

"How did you know that?"

She smiled. "You're new in town, and Joshua is the first person strangers see when they come to town. My name is Louisa; this is my place."

She stuck her hand out like a man, and he shook it. She had a firm grip—firmer than that of a lot of men Clint had known.

"Clint Adams."

"Mr. Adams. Well, I think that the food and coffee are as advertised—but that's my opinion. You'll have to form your own."

"All I need for that is a table."

She smiled again, making herself pretty, and said, "Follow me."

She had black hair and eyebrows, brown eyes, and dark skin. He followed her to a table, and she said, "I'll bring the coffee first and then your dinner."

"But I haven't ordered."

She smiled and said, "Leave that to me, Mr. Adams."

"If I'm going to leave myself in your hands," he said, "you might as well call me Clint."

"I don't think you'll be disappointed, Clint," she said, then added, "with anything."

As he watched her walk away, he didn't think he would be disappointed either.

He was on his second pot of coffee when she came out of the kitchen with a tray laden with food.

"Here," she said. "You've waited long enough."

"As long as it's worth the wait."

Setting the food on the table, she said, "That'll be for you to say, and only you."

Judging from the look and smell of the food, it would be worth the wait. She had brought a bowl of stew, filled with meat and vegetables, and some hot biscuits.

"When you're finished here," she said, "I'll bring out a steak."

"Don't you think this will be enough?" he asked.

"You look like a hungry man."

And he was.

He polished off the stew, enjoying every bite of it, and

when he was done he used the biscuits to clean the plate. When she brought the steak it filled the plate, steaming and running with blood, and she brought another basket of biscuits.

"You don't look especially busy," he said. "Will you sit with me and tell me about your town?"

She smiled. "I'd rather tell you about me—and hear about you."

"Will the cook mind if you sit?"

She sat opposite him and said, "I *am* the cook."

They talked while he ate his steak. She'd been born in California and came north with her family when she was thirteen. Her father and mother had begun this restaurant when there wasn't much else here but a few buildings and named it after her. Her mother had died of a fever when she was fifteen, and her father had been killed by a drunk when she was twenty.

"I've lived here and run this restaurant alone for the past thirteen years."

"There must be men around," Clint said. "And you haven't married?"

"Never found the right man. You?"

"I travel too much. Wouldn't be fair to a woman to marry her."

"But . . . you've known women, haven't you?"

"Some."

She smiled.

"A lot, I'll bet."

He smiled now and said, "Some. And what about you? Any men?"

"A few," she said. "Now and then. Not many."

He believed her.

"And not from the town," she added. "That would be too complicated."

"Strangers?"

She nodded.

"Like you."

"Are you saying what I think you're saying?"

"I think so," she said. "There's no pretense, no . . . false wishes involved. I don't want you to take me with you when you leave. Do you find me attractive?"

"Very."

"And you'll be able to eat here for free, as long as you're in town."

Clint made a face and said, "That would make me feel too much like a whore."

She looked startled. "I didn't mean—"

"I know you didn't," he said. He pushed his empty plate away, drained his coffee cup and set it down, then pushed back his chair.

"Are you leaving?" she asked.

"Yes."

"What about—"

"I'll think about it, Louisa," he said.

She put her chin in her hands and said, "Don't take too long. I wouldn't want to waste too much time."

He grinned and said, "I'll let you know." Then he left.

Normally, Clint didn't mind aggressive women, but Louisa's attitude toward sex with a stranger was something he was going to have to get used to.

Not that he had never had sex with a stranger before— even on a moment's notice—but he'd never had a woman put it to him so . . . succinctly.

Again, Clint decided to bypass the bath and went straight to the fair. He wanted to see Bat and Bat's wrestler.

THREE

The fair wasn't large. There appeared to be eight or ten wagons, with some sort of act set up in front of each. There was even a sharpshooter act. Clint could hear the shooting going on, but he was more interested in the wrestler. He asked someone where the wrestler was set up and was pointed in the right direction. He was at the farthest end of the fairgrounds.

Along the way he passed tables laden with food, mostly cakes and pies that seemed to be for sale. He purchased a small piece of apple pie and held it in his hand while he ate it. He passed several tents along the way as well.

When he reached the wrestler's tent there was a match already in progress.

There were two men inside a circle drawn on the ground, and around them were the spectators, cheering one or both of them on. Clint had no doubt that side bets had been made. That was probably where Bat expected to make most of their money.

Clint watched with interest as the huge, masked Oregon Strangler grappled with a man almost his size. The challenger, however, seemed to be tiring, and before long the masked man upended him, dumped him on his back, and pinned him.

"Beaten in two rounds," Bat Masterson shouted, stepping into the circle.

Clint smiled at the sight of his friend. Always the picture of sartorial splendor, this time was no different. He wore a dark suit with a boiled white shirt, and on his head was his bowler. In his left hand he held a cane with a silver tip. Clint also knew that there'd be a gun in a shoulder rig underneath the jacket.

"Two rounds," Bat said again, "and a good try. Let him up, Strangler."

The masked man rose and helped the fallen man to his feet. He extended his hand to his vanquished opponent, but the man sneered and slunk away, holding his back. Some of his friends left with him.

"Any other takers?" Bat called.

The people in the crowd looked at each other, but no one stepped up.

"Then that concludes today's show, ladies and gentlemen," Bat said. "Go and enjoy the rest of the fair, and come back tomorrow."

Bat turned and slapped his wrestler on the back. As he did so he spotted Clint, squinted his eyes, and then smiled.

"Well, I'll be—" he said.

Clint stepped forward, his hand extended. "Bat."

"How the hell are you, Clint?" Bat asked, clasping his friend's hand tightly. "And what the hell are you doing up here?"

"Same as you, Bat," Clint said. "Trying to make a living. I hear you've got a good thing going here."

"Not bad, Clint," Bat said, "as scams go. Come on, come inside and I'll introduce you to my boy."

The masked Strangler had already gone into the tent, and Clint and Bat followed. The big man had removed his mask, and now he turned to face them.

"Clint, meet Lenny Younger. Lenny, this is as good a friend as I've got, Clint Adams."

"A pleasure, Mr. Adams," Younger said. He put out a huge hand and Clint took it. The boy was immensely powerful, but he didn't make a point of displaying it. His handshake was firm, but not overly so.

"Get dressed, son, and we'll go to town and have a drink with Clint."

"You know I don't drink, Bat," Lenny Younger said reproachfully.

"Oh, that's right, I keep forgetting," Bat said. He looked at Clint and said, "I promised the kid's ma I'd look after him. That includes keeping him safe from things like 'demon whiskey.' That was the only way she'd let him come with me."

"From where?"

"Virginia," Lenny Younger said. "My home is in Virginia, Mr. Adams."

Younger seemed to be about twenty, although he could have passed for less. He was also incredibly soft-spoken and polite. He was not what Clint would have expected to find under the mask.

"Well, get dressed anyway, boy, and we'll go to town and get you . . . something."

"Why don't you and Mr. Adams go ahead, Bat. I'll just stay here and rest awhile."

"Rest?" Bat said, laughing. "Rest, the boy says. He never gets tired, Clint."

"That's what I heard," Clint said, but, looking at the boy's face, he doubted that was true. Maybe he didn't get tired in the conventional sense—not physically—but one look at his face told Clint that the boy was almost exhausted in other ways.

"Okay, kid," Bat said. "You take it easy, and Clint and I will go and do some catching up."

"Sure, Bat." Younger looked at Clint and said, "It was very nice to meet you, sir."

"And you, Lenny," Clint said.

"Come on, Clint," Bat said. "Let me show you the wonders of Placerville."

FOUR

The saloon was a little busier this time than it had been earlier, and there were girls working the floor.

"This is the best the town has to offer," Bat said.

"Where have you been eating?" Clint asked.

"The hotel dining room, why?"

"Nothing."

That probably meant that Louisa hadn't tried her proposition out on Bat. Clint wondered if she'd consider Lenny Younger too young for her.

"Two beers, Tom," Bat said to the bartender. It figured that Bat knew the bartender's name. He probably also knew the names of the two girls working the floor.

The bartender brought the beers, and Clint followed Bat to a table in the back.

Bat gave Clint a quick rundown of his wrestling scam.

"When I saw this kid I knew he was a natural. It's not only his size, but the kid doesn't seem to get tired."

"I've heard that."

"Where?"

Clint inclined his head toward the bartender.

"Ah, Tom. He was one of the first ones to try the kid. Lenny pinned him in a minute."

"If you don't mind my saying so, Bat, the kid looks pretty tired to me."

"No, I'm telling you, he doesn't get tired."

"Maybe not while he's wrestling, but . . . How long have you two been doing this?"

"A few months," Bat said with a shrug.

"And how are *you* feeling?"

"Me? I'm fine. I'm not as young as I used to be, but who is? Maybe I'm feeling a little bit tired—"

"Ah-hah!"

"Ah-hah what?"

"You're tired and you're not wrestling. Imagine how he feels."

Bat opened his mouth to reply, then stopped and assumed a thoughtful expression.

"Maybe you're right," he said. "Maybe I've been pushing the kid too hard."

"Maybe . . ."

"Maybe I should give him some rest."

Clint nodded and said, "Maybe . . ."

"Maybe . . . I should bring him here and turn him over to one of these girls."

Clint thought about that, then nodded and said, "Yeah, maybe . . ."

"Hey, Liz," Bat called out to one of the girls.

As she approached the table, Clint saw that she hadn't been a "girl" in some time. She was probably close to forty, a big-bodied woman with firm breasts and ass.

"Hi, Bat," she said, sliding into his lap. "Who's your friend?"

"Never mind him," Bat said. "He never pays for his women."

"Well, I can see why," she said, giving Clint a flirtatious look.

"Liz, what would you do with a twenty-year-old boy who's six foot eight and over three hundred pounds?"

Liz drew back so she could look right into Bat's face. "Are you serious?"

"Very serious."

"Twenty years old?"

"That's right."

Her eyes widened as she repeated, "Six foot eight and three hundred pounds?"

"That's right," Bat said. "And none of it is fat."

"What would I do with him?"

Bat nodded, and Clint waited with interest for her answer.

Liz licked her full lips and, grinning, said, "I'd eat him alive!"

Bat and Clint were going back to the fair to try and bring Lenny back to the saloon with them.

"What's more relaxing than being with a woman?" Bat asked.

Clint thought for a moment but couldn't come up with anything.

"I mean, it's exciting," Bat said, "and then it's relaxing, you know?"

"I know," Clint said. "Uh, do you think Lenny's ever been with a woman before?"

Bat thought for a moment, then said, "I, uh, don't know."

"Do you think a saloon girl is the ideal first woman for a farm boy?"

"Well," Bat said, "I'm sure she's experienced enough to handle it the right way."

"Who was your first woman?"

"Damned if I remember," Bat said. "I think I was drunk at the time. What about you?"

"I was . . . fourteen or fifteen, I think."

"Really?"

"Yeah," Clint said. "She was an older woman—she was eighteen. Long blond hair, big tits, wide hips—boy, she was comfortable to lie on."

"How long did it last?"

"I think it was over almost before it started, but we tried a few more times after that."

"Did anyone know?"

"Sure," Clint said, "all of the other boys in class. I'll bet twenty or thirty boys under sixteen lost their virginity to her."

"What was her name?"

"Damned if I can remember."

When they got to the tent they looked inside and found Younger sitting on a rickety wooden chair, reading.

"What's he reading?" Clint asked.

Bat shrugged and stepped into the tent.

"What are you reading, Lenny?"

Lenny looked up, surprised to see them. He looked like a boy who had been caught with his hand in the cookie jar.

"Uh . . ." He started to hide the book behind his back, then changed his mind and held it up. "It's just the Bible."

"The Bible, huh?" Bat said.

"Yes, sir."

Bat and Clint exchanged a glance and Clint started to back out of the tent.

"I don't think this is such a good idea after all," he started to say.

"Sure it is," Bat said. "Come on, Lenny, we're taking you out."

"Out?" Lenny Younger asked. "Out where?"

Bat grabbed the kid's arm and pulled him to his feet.

"You'll see, kid," he said. "You'll see."

FIVE

As Bat Masterson pushed Lenny Younger into the saloon, Clint Adams still wasn't sure this was a good idea. If Younger *was* a virgin, and a Bible reader, he might not be too receptive to what Bat was trying to give him—and Clint felt responsible for it. He was the one who'd convinced Bat that the kid needed some rest, but maybe this was the wrong kind of rest.

When they entered the saloon, Lenny's size caught the attention of everyone in the room, men and women alike.

"Bat," Younger said, uncomfortably, "I've never been in a saloon. . . ."

"Don't worry, kid," Bat said. "There's a first time for everything."

"If Mother found out—"

"We won't tell her, boy. Come on, I want you to meet someone."

Bat walked Lenny over to the same table he and Clint had been sitting at before and waved at Liz to come over.

Clint sat down opposite Younger and watched.

"Oh, my God, Bat!" Liz said, her eyes wide as she stared at Younger. "You weren't kidding."

"Lenny, meet Liz."

"H-hello . . ." Lenny said nervously.

"Oooh, honey," Liz said, sliding into Lenny's lap, "you are a big one, aren't you?"

The poor kid, Clint thought. He didn't have the faintest idea of what to do. Liz was wiggling her butt in his lap and pushing her breasts into his face, and he wouldn't have been human if he didn't respond—but that response seemed to horrify him.

"Oh, baby," Liz said, wiggling her ass some more, "I feel something. . . . Ooh, God, it's so big. . . ."

When she reached down with her hand to grab him, Lenny suddenly sprang to his feet, spilling Liz onto the table. Only Clint's speed kept the table from falling as he grabbed Liz and rescued her.

"Hey!" she shouted.

"Harlot!" Lenny Younger shouted, his face red with rage. "Servant of Satan!"

"Lenny . . ." Bat said, looking totally shocked by the boy's behavior.

"I have to leave, Bat," Lenny said. "I *have* to leave."

With that Lenny actually ran from the saloon, with everyone staring after him.

Clint had his arms around Liz, and he helped her off the table and to her feet.

"Well," she said, a little breathless, "what's wrong with him?"

"It's not your fault, Liz," Clint replied. "He's just not good with women."

"Well, that's a shame." Clint still had his arms around her, and she snuggled close to him and asked, "I don't think you have that problem though, do you?"

He slid his hands down her back to her solid butt, gave her a pat, and said, "Not usually."

She slid her right forefinger down his nose and over his lips. "Too bad you don't pay."

He smiled, and she turned to Bat.

"I'm sorry, Liz," Bat said.

"You can make it up to me . . . later," Liz said. She touched Bat's face and then walked away.

"Bat . . ." Clint began.

"I know," Bat said, "You were right. This wasn't the way." He shook his head in awe. "Did you see the way she flew out of his lap and onto the table? If you hadn't caught her . . ."

"Have you ever seen him lose his temper like that before?" Clint asked.

"Never," Bat said. "I knew he read the Bible from time to time, but I never would have expected an outburst like that. What did he call her? A harlot?"

"And a 'servant of Satan,' " Clint added.

"Jesus," Bat said, "I will have to make it up to Liz. It's going to take a lot of energy."

"And a lot of money," Clint reminded him.

"That too. You want another beer?"

"Is there anything else to do in this town?"

"Not if you don't pay for women," Bat said.

"Don't you think you should go after Lenny?"

"No," Bat said. "Let the kid cool down a bit on his own. If I know him, he'll be apologizing to me later."

"All right then," Clint said, "I guess my only choices are to turn in or have another beer with you."

"Maybe we can find a deck of cards."

As Bat went to the bar for two more beers, Clint realized that he had a third choice after all.

Louisa.

He had one more beer with Bat but turned down another one.

"Turning in after all?" Bat asked.

"No," Clint said, "I just remembered another option. Why don't you make your apologies to Liz."

"She won't be free for a few hours yet. I guess I'll just sit here and wait. What's your other option?"

Clint grinned and said, "The kind I don't pay for."

SIX

When Clint reached Louisa's she was just locking the door from the inside. She looked out at him through the glass before opening it.

"Did you come for something to eat?"

"No."

He stepped inside, and she closed and locked the door. There was no light in the interior.

"Follow me," she said.

Clint followed her through the darkened restaurant to the kitchen—which was also dark—and through the kitchen to a stairway. He followed her up the stairway to a door and through it. They were in what looked like a living room, and she led him to a second room—a bedroom.

She turned and looked at him, then began to unbutton her blouse.

"Of course," she said, "I haven't had a chance to bathe."

"As a matter of fact," Clint said, unbuttoning his own shirt, "neither have I."

Her body was as firm as it had promised to be.

Her breasts were large and firm, and as she sat astride him, he held them in his hands. He was buried deeply inside of her, and she was riding him, her hands braced against his chest as she rose up and down on him. He slid his hands from her breasts around to her back and pulled her down to him, so he could suck her nipples. She moaned when he scraped her nipples with his teeth, and then he slid his hands down her back to cup her buttocks. As he pulled her to him, he rose up off the bed to meet her, and she gasped at how deeply he penetrated her.

"Oh, God . . ." she gasped into his ear. "Oh, yes, harder, harder . . . faster . . ."

She began to move more quickly, and he quickened his pace to match hers. Before long she was bouncing on top of him, in the throes of her orgasm, her head thrown back, her eyes tightly closed, the cords on her neck standing out. . . .

Then he exploded inside of her. . . .

"Wake up."

Clint came awake instantly, aware that she was shaking him.

"You have to go."

"What? Why?"

"I have to get up early and make breakfast for half the town."

"What time is it?"

"Almost midnight," Louisa said. She leaned over and kissed him, her nipples brushing his chest. "I'm sorry, but I can't sleep with someone else in the bed with me."

Clint did not get insulted. He had known women like that before. Even he himself preferred to sleep alone, truth be told.

He stood up and got dressed while she watched.

"I like watching men get dressed."

"I don't mind you watching."

She had noticed that he dressed without any self-consciousness whatsoever. This was a man very confident in himself, and she liked that.

"Next time," he said at the door, "I'll take a bath first."

She smiled and said, "So will I."

Clint used the back door to leave, realizing that it would stay unlocked unless Louisa came down to lock it. On his way to the hotel he noticed that the saloon was still going strong. He wondered if Bat were still waiting for Liz, or if she had already finished work.

He hoped Bat had the energy to make his apology a sincere one.

Liz had both of her hands in Bat's hair while Bat's tongue worked on her. She moaned, slid her tongue between her lips, and then cried out, tensing her body.

"Ohh, Bat," she said, "you're the only one who can make me do that. . . ."

Bat rose over her, ignoring her whore talk. It came naturally to her. He slid into her easily, and she wrapped her legs around his waist.

This was the second stage of the apology. . . .

The third stage of the apology came as he was leaving. He dropped the money on her dresser on the way out.

"Thank you, Bat dear," she said from the bed. "You're forgiven."

"Good night, Liz."

Bat left by the back exit of the saloon, unaware of the fact that the door remained unlocked behind him.

SEVEN

The man tried the back door and found it unlocked. He opened it, entered, and closed it behind him. He made his way down the hall to the back stairway and ascended quickly and silently to the second floor.

When he reached his destination, the woman was lying in bed, uncovered. She was naked, and in the moonlight that came streaming in through the window he took a moment to look at her. She was lying on her back with one leg raised. Her breasts were flattened out against her chest, but he could see that they were impressive, firm and with large nipples. In the moonlight, he could even see her belly and the dark hole that was her navel.

Having taken enough time to look at her, he moved toward the bed. She was either a light sleeper or she was never really asleep at all.

She sat up in bed and asked, "Did you forget something?"

He slid onto the bed and reached for her.

"Hey, wait!" she said. "Who are you!"

He took her throat in his hands and pushed her down onto her back. He placed his knee on her, just below her breasts, and began to squeeze her neck. She had already lost her breath from the pressure of his knee, and now she was fighting for air. As his hands closed on her throat, tighter and tighter, she began to beat on him with her fists, having no effect. Even though she was a large woman, he was just too big and strong for her to hurt.

He leaned on her, straightening his arms, and he felt something give beneath his knee. He ignored it and continued to squeeze her throat until her squirming stopped.

He removed his hands from her neck and stood up beside the bed. He reached over and pushed her head on the pillow, then watched it flop over and stay there. Her breasts were still, indicating that she was not breathing. He took a moment to pass his large hand over her breasts, which were still warm. She might have still been alive, except that when he pinched her nipples there was no reaction whatsoever.

Satisfied that she was dead, he left the same way he had come in.

Downstairs he paused by the door for a moment, but there was no way for him to go out through it and lock it behind him. He was going to have to leave it unlocked behind him. But, then, it had been unlocked to begin with, hadn't it?

He left the building and, for all his size, melted into the darkness of the alley.

EIGHT

In the morning Clint went to the livery and found plenty of work waiting for him. He had stopped by Louisa's cafe for breakfast first, but her place had been closed. He figured she'd had to sleep late after last night.

He took that as a compliment.

"People started coming in yesterday, not long after you first put up the posters," Joshua told him.

"Doesn't the town have a regular gunsmith?"

"No," Joshua said. "If they can't fix it themselves, they just put it aside and wait for someone who can. Look."

Joshua walked Clint back to his rig and showed him five or six guns that had been brought in for him to fix.

"Do you know what's wrong with all of them?"

"Sure I do. . . . Well, I *did* ask, and I *do* know what's wrong, but . . . maybe I don't know which problem goes with which gun . . . exactly."

"I see." There were four rifles and two handguns. "Don't worry, Joshua, I can figure out what's wrong with them."

"Good," Joshua said, smiling. "Then we can start making money."

"Right."

"And you can, you know, charge them a little more than you normally would."

"Why?"

"Well, like I said, there's no gunsmith in town. If you don't fix it, it ain't gonna get fixed."

"Joshua," Clint said, "I'm not overcharging anyone. I'll charge my usual fees, and not a penny more."

"What are you, totally honest?"

"Totally."

Joshua scratched his head. "I never met a man who was totally honest."

"Why don't you let me get to work, Joshua."

"Sure," the other man said, and he walked off, still scratching his head.

Clint climbed into the back of his wagon and started sorting the guns. Some of the problems would be obvious, some would take a little more time, but eventually he'd find them all and fix them. By then maybe he'd have some more business walk in. Later on he wanted to find Bat and see if he had spoken to Lenny Younger yet about last night.

Lenny Younger sat in his tent, rubbing the sleep from his face. Across the way Bat Masterson was just rousing himself. Both had slept late. Lenny stood up, went outside, and got a pail of water. He brought it back into the tent and put it down in front of Bat's pallet. Bat was sitting up at that point, and he looked up at Lenny, who didn't say a word.

"Morning, Lenny."

"Good morning, Bat," Lenny said, sitting back down on his pallet.

Bat stood up and carried the pail of water to a wooden table. He set it down and started washing his face and torso.

While he was drying himself, he turned to Lenny and said, "About last night, kid . . ."

"Forget it, Bat."

"I'm really sorry," Bat said. "I didn't mean to—"

"I said forget it."

"I was worried when I came in and you weren't here," Bat said. He dropped the towel on the table and walked over to where Lenny was sitting. "I thought *I* got in late last night. Where were you?"

"I was walking."

"Where?"

"Just walking."

"Kid, I hope you can forgive me—"

"Bat," Lenny said, looking up at the older man, "I want to go home."

"Now, kid—"

"No," Lenny said, "you can't talk me out of it. I want my share of the money and I want to go home."

"To Virginia?"

"Yes."

"Back to the farm, kid?"

"That's my home."

"I know it, but—is this about last night?"

"Some of it," Lenny said. "But mostly I just want to go home. Can I have my money or can't I, Bat?"

"Sure you can, kid, sure you can. It's in the bank. We'll have to wait until it opens. Do you want to leave today?"

"Yes."

"Kid, I wish you'd change your mind."

"Why do you always call me 'kid'?" Lenny asked. "How come you never call me by my name?"

"Lenny, look, I'm sorry."

"Let's just get my money so I can go home."

"You want to make your own way home?"

"Yes."

"You don't want me to come with you?"

"No."

Bat knew that without him the kid would get totally lost.

"You really aren't going to forgive me, are you?" Bat asked.

Lenny didn't answer.

"All right," Bat said. "Let's get dressed and get over to the bank. We can be there when it opens."

NINE

Sheriff Ken Birch awoke on the cot in cell number one. He sat up and scratched his bare, sunken chest. The forty-three-year-old sheriff was about six feet tall, but he barely weighed a hundred and forty pounds. Once he had weighed more than two hundred, but that was a long time ago. Also, once he had been a fine lawman, but that had also been a long time ago. Now he was hiding in a small town up north, trying to keep out of harm's way, while doing the only thing he knew how to do—keep the peace. Of course, in a town like Placerville, peace was an easy thing to keep, because there was so much of it. That was why he was able to sleep late.

He dragged his feet into his office and put on a pot of coffee. He was rubbing his face with both hands when the door opened.

"Sheriff!"

Birch put his hands down and looked at Sid Denning, the owner of the saloon. Denning was in his thirties, and he had built the saloon about four years ago. He had come to Placerville with four girls and a bartender, and now he owned the only saloon in town. He still had one bartender and four girls, but they weren't the ones he had come to town with—all except for one of the girls.

"Morning, Sid," Birch said. "Coffee?"

"No, thanks."

"What can I do for you?"

"Sorry to interrupt you before your first cup of coffee, Ken," Denning said, "but I've got a problem. A big one."

"Big enough to keep me from my coffee?"

"I'm afraid so."

"You don't look so good, Sid," Birch said. "Tell me what's wrong."

"One of my girls is dead."

"What?"

"Liz Abel."

"Liz?" Birch's face betrayed his disbelief. "I didn't know she was sick."

Denning made a face.

"She wasn't sick, Ken," he said impatiently. "Somebody killed her."

"Killed her?"

"Looks like he choked her to death. Might even have raped her."

"Liz? Why would he have to rape her?"

"I don't know, Ken," Denning said. "You're the sheriff. Are you coming?"

"Sure, sure," Sheriff Birch said. "Just let me get my shirt and I'll come with you."

With a sense of dread, Birch pulled on his shirt. He'd been sheriff here for five years and he'd never had to deal with anything but drunks.

Murder scared the shit out of him.

Joshua came into the livery while Clint was working.

"Some excitement over to the saloon," he said.

"What kind of excitement?"

"Heard that one of the girls was killed last night."

Clint looked up from what he was doing and said, "Killed?"

"That's what they say."

"One of the saloon girls?"

Joshua nodded.

"Did you hear the name?"

"Sure," Joshua said. "Liz Abel."

"Liz?"

"Big black-haired girl," Joshua said.

"I think I met her last night," Clint said. He put down the gun he was working on. "I guess I'll go over and find out what happened."

"What if we get some more customers?" Joshua asked.

"Just take care of them as expertly as you took care of the others."

TEN

By the time Clint reached the saloon, a crowd had formed outside. He elbowed his way through to the front in time to see a man with a badge come out the front door. The man was ordinarily sallow faced, but now he was as white as a sheet. Clint immediately had the feeling that the lawman was in over his head.

Behind him another man came out. A quick question to the man next to him told Clint who the two men were.

"What are you going to do about this, Sheriff?" Sid Denning demanded.

"I—I'll do what I can, Sid."

"And what's that going to be?" Denning asked. "One of my girls is dead, Ken. I want the maniac who killed her to hang."

"Well, Sid," the sheriff said, trying to assert himself, "before we can hang him we have to find him."

"Well, find him!" Denning said.

"I don't know who I'm looking for, Sid," Sheriff Birch said. "Come on, give me a break here."

"I can help you," a man said, stepping forward. In fact, it was the man Clint had been standing beside.

Birch squinted at the man until he identified him.

"Sam Warner?"

"I saw the killer, Sheriff," Warner said. "At least I think I did."

Sam Warner was a man in his forties, small of stature but with a surprisingly loud voice—so loud that everyone was hearing what he had to say.

"Well, who was it, Sam?" Sid Denning asked.

"Sid," Birch said, "if you don't mind, I'll handle the questions." The sheriff looked at Sam Warner and said, "Well, who was it, Sam?"

"I didn't see his face," Warner said apologetically, "but he was a big man—a *real* big man. Probably six and a half feet tall."

"How many six and a half foot tall men do we have in town?" Denning asked, but Birch ignored him.

"Sam, suppose you tell me exactly what you saw."

"Sure, Sheriff," Warner said. "I saw—"

"Not here," Birch said. "Come over to my office."

"I'll come, too," Sid Denning said, but the sheriff stopped him.

"Stay here, Sid. I'll have a couple of men come over and take the body to the undertaker's."

"I want to hear what Sam has to say," Denning complained.

"I'll let you know what he says," Birch said. "Stay here, all right?"

"Sure, sure," Denning said, "I'll stay here. You just find out who killed my girl . . . Sheriff."

Birch and Warner made their way through the crowd and continued on to the sheriff's office.

Clint moved forward and asked Sid Denning, "Which girl was it, Mr. Denning?"

Denning looked at Clint and tried to place him but couldn't. He answered anyway.

"Liz," he said.

"Tall, dark-haired gal? Closing in on forty?"

"Closing in hell," Denning said. "She was close to forty when we got here, and that was four years ago. She was the last of the original girls I brought with me. She was my *best* girl, too, and now some maniac's killed her."

"How?"

"Strangled her, looks like," Denning said. "Say, what's your interest? Who are you?"

"I got to town yesterday," Clint said, "but I met Liz last night in your place."

Denning took a closer look at Clint, and Clint knew that the man was mentally measuring. Clint didn't come close to six and a half feet, but he knew someone who did.

Could Lenny Younger have had something to do with this? Or was he just in the wrong place at the wrong time?

The crowd started to discuss who in town was that big, and Clint eased away to go and warn Bat. Soon enough someone would think of the big masked wrestler at the fair. And then somebody would mention a rope.

That's all it took to turn a crowd into a lynch mob.

As Clint reached the northern end of town, he saw Bat and Lenny walking toward him. In a moment, they'd be in sight on the main street.

"Bat!" Clint called, trotting up to stop them from turning the corner.

"Morning, Clint." Clint noticed that Bat and Lenny didn't seem to be in a very good mood. In fact, they didn't seem to be speaking to each other.

"Bat, hold up there."

"We're on the way to the bank, Clint," Bat said. "Lenny here wants to break off the partnership, take his money, and go home."

"I don't think that's such a good idea," Clint said. In

order to get to the bank they'd have to pass the saloon—
and the crowd.

"That's what I told him, but he insists."

"No, that's not what I mean," Clint said. Lenny was
starting to move past him, and Clint took hold of his arm.
It was like grabbing a tree trunk.

"Lenny, where were you last night?" Clint asked.

"In the tent."

"All night?"

Lenny looked at Bat and then said, "I walked around
some and then went to sleep in the tent."

Clint looked at Bat and dropped Lenny's arm.

"Was he asleep when you got to the tent?"

"No, he came in later, after I fell asleep. What's this all
about, Clint?"

"Somebody killed that saloon girl, Bat."

"Which saloon girl?"

"Liz," Clint said, looking at Lenny to see how he'd take
the news. It didn't seem to faze him one way or the other.

"Somebody killed Liz?" Bat asked in shock.

"Yep," Clint said. "Somebody strangled her."

"Jesus!"

"Bat, let's go get my money," Lenny said, and he
started past Clint again. Clint took hold of his arm again.

"Lenny, don't—"

He stopped when Lenny pulled his arm from his grasp
with ease.

"Please don't grab me again, Mr. Adams. I don't like it."
There was no menace in Lenny's voice, but his size was
menacing enough.

"Lenny, just hold on a minute," Clint said softly. "I've
got something—"

"I'm goin' to the bank for my money," Lenny said, and
he started walking.

"Clint, what is it?" Bat asked.

Clint turned to Bat and said, "Somebody identified the killer as a man six and a half feet tall."

"So?"

"So how many men in town are that big, Bat?" Clint asked.

Bat frowned and said, "Only Lenny. I see what you mean."

"There's a crowd in front of the saloon just begging to become a lynch mob," Clint said. "We've got to keep them from seeing the boy!"

Suddenly there was the sound of shouting, and Clint and Bat quickly moved around the corner to see what was happening.

The mob from the saloon had obviously spotted Lenny and people were running toward him. The leader of the mob was Sid Denning.

Poor Lenny was rooted to where he stood, not knowing what the hell was going on.

"Jesus!" Bat said. "They'll tear him to pieces!"

ELEVEN

Clint and Bat broke into a run, but it was clear that the mob was going to reach Lenny before they did. They did the only thing they could do to save the kid.

They drew their guns.

"Fire over their heads!" Clint shouted.

"Right!"

They both started firing over the heads of the crowd members. At first the men were shocked into stopping, and they looked around to see where the shots were coming from. When Clint and Bat fired again, they were jarred into action, and they scattered. Men were running every which way for cover.

Clint and Bat reached Lenny, each taking hold of one arm.

"What's happening, Bat?" Lenny asked.

"I'll explain it later, Lenny," Bat said. "Right now we've got to get you out of here."

"But . . . the bank," Lenny said.

"We'll worry about the bank later, Lenny," Bat said. "Let's go!"

They turned him around, and the three of them started running back the way they had come. Clint and Bat fired another shot each, just to keep the mob from following right away.

"You know the sheriff's going to be after us now," Clint said to Bat.

"I know."

"The sheriff?" Lenny asked. "What for?"

"Later, Lenny, later," Bat said. To Clint he said, "We have to find someplace safe to talk."

"You've been here longer than I have," Clint said. "Lead the way."

"Yeah," Bat said, "right." He thought for a moment and then said, "Right, follow me."

In the sheriff's office, Birch was listening to Sam Warner's story. Warner was the last one to have left the saloon, and he was getting some air before he went home to his wife, who was going to give him hell.

"I was across the street from the saloon when I see this big feller come out of the alley and start to turn toward the north end of town."

"And that's all you know about him?" Birch asked. "That he was big?"

"That's all, Sheriff."

"But . . . you didn't see him do anything?"

"No."

"Jesus, Sam," Birch said, "you should have kept your mouth shut in front of that mob out there."

"Why?"

"Because they won't need much to turn them into a lynch mob, especially with Sid Denning bellyaching about his best girl being killed. Jesus!"

"Maybe nothing will happen, Sheriff," Warner started to say, but suddenly there was the sound of shouting from outside.

"Now what the hell . . ." Birch said. He got up from his chair to look out the window, but before he got there he heard shooting.

"Shit!" he said, and he rushed to the window. By the time he looked outside, all he saw was men running everywhere, diving for cover.

"Stay here," he told Warner, and he went outside.

"What's going on?" he shouted to the man nearest him. He was a handyman named Will Early.

"They're shooting at us!"

"Who is?"

"I don't know."

"Well, why are they shooting at you?"

"I don't know."

Birch scowled.

"Will, where's Denning?"

"I think he ran across the street," Early said, from where he was crouched behind the horse trough.

Birch stepped into the street, which was completely empty now.

"Sid Denning!" he shouted.

"Sheriff."

Birch turned and saw Denning stand up. He had been hiding behind some barrels in front of the general store.

"What the hell is going on?" Birch demanded.

Denning came out from behind the barrel tentatively and stepped into the street.

"We saw him, Sheriff."

"Saw who?"

"The killer."

"Who was it?"

"I don't know," Denning said, "but he was big."

"What makes you think he's the killer?"

"Well . . . he was big," Denning said again.

"Do you know who he was?"

"No."

"Was he shooting at you?"

"No," Denning said, "that was Bat Masterson and another feller."

"Masterson?" Birch said, swallowing hard. "Why was he shooting at you?"

"He was trying to protect that big feller," Denning said. "You know what I think?"

"What?"

"I think that feller was his wrestler—you know, the one they call the Oregon Strangler." Suddenly, Denning became agitated and said, "See, they even *call* him a strangler."

"Jesus," Birch said, trying to shake the feeling that he was in over his head. First a dead body, then a six and a half foot killer, and now Bat Masterson.

"What are you going to do, Sheriff?" Denning asked.

Birch looked at Denning and decided to take his growing anger and confusion out on him.

"First thing I'm gonna do is get you and these other crazy fools off the street!"

"You're chasing *us*?" Denning asked in disbelief. "You're going to need our help, especially if you're after Bat Masterson and that friend of his."

"Yeah," Birch said, "I saw how brave you all were a minute ago."

"Sheriff—"

"Look, Sid, if Bat Masterson was shooting at you, some of you would be dead now. Was anyone hurt?"

Both he and Denning looked around as the men began slowly coming out from their cover. No one looked as if he had been so much as scratched.

"No," Birch said, answering his own question. "Chances

are he was shooting over your heads to scatter you. And you all obliged him."

"Sheriff—"

"Get indoors, Sid!" Birch shouted. "And that goes for the rest of you. Go on about your business. I'll find Bat Masterson and talk to him."

"Sheriff—" Denning said for the third time.

"Move, dammit," Birch shouted, "before I decide to do some shooting."

Denning looked at Birch with surprise clear on his face. Obviously, he didn't think the lawman had this kind of behavior in him.

It was a surprise to Sheriff Ken Birch as well.

TWELVE

Clint was surprised that Bat was heading back to the fairgrounds.

"Bat," he said, "this is going to be the first place they look."

"I know," Bat said.

Clint fell silent, figuring Bat must have a plan when they kept walking past the tent he and Lenny shared. Instead, Bat led them to a tent at the far end of the grounds.

"Cory, honey?" he called.

There was some movement inside the tent, and then a woman stepped out. She had flaming red hair and was wearing an outfit made of flimsy scarves that showed a lot of flesh between her impressive bosom and her waist. The belly that showed was not flat, but it was smooth, and the navel was a dark shadow.

"This is Cory Evers," Bat said. "She goes by the name of Little Egypt. She's one of them exotic dancers."

"Exotic dancer?" Clint asked.

"Yes," Cory said, and she gave him a small sample. Her hips moved and her belly undulated as if it had a life of its own. Lenny stared at her navel for a minute, then looked away, red-faced.

Clint did not look away, and when he looked at Cory's face he found that she was looking right at him.

"I wear a black wig," she said, "because there aren't many red-haired Egyptians."

"The marks—I mean, the customers—look right past the fact that she's pale-skinned, not dark," Bat said. "All they can see is—well, what you see."

The top she wore was skimpy enough to show the smooth slopes of her full breasts, and for a moment Clint forgot why they were there.

"Cory, we need a place to stay for a while."

"To stay?" she repeated, frowning.

"To hide," Clint said.

"What's wrong?"

"A woman was killed last night in town," Bat said, "and the townspeople seem to think Lenny did it."

"Me?" Lenny asked. "They think I killed somebody? Is that why they were running at me? Is that why we're running away?"

"That's why, kid," Bat said. "What do you say, Cory? I figure yours will be the last tent they search."

"Sure, Bat," Cory said, "go on in. But introduce me to your friend first."

"Sure," Bat said. "Cory, this is Clint Adams."

"Hello, Clint."

She put out her hand, and Clint shook it. Being an arm's length from her was heady. She appeared to be about twenty-eight. If she was thirty, she was wearing it very well.

"I'll go and talk to Pop," Cory said.

"Pop?" Clint asked.

"Pop Hingle," Bat said. "He owns this traveling fair."

"Sometimes we call it a carnival," Cory said. "Pop'll be on your side, Bat. We stick up for each other around here."

"All right, Cory," Bat said. "I'll trust your judgment."

Cory went over and stood in front of Lenny, who was still looking away from her.

"Who could think that Lenny could kill someone?" she asked. "He's so gentle." She got up on her toes and kissed Lenny on the cheek, which turned his face a fiery red. "Don't worry, big boy. Bat and his friend, Clint, will get things straightened out."

"Thanks for your help, Cory."

"I'll be back in a while," she said, and she ran off, her whispy scarves swirling.

THIRTEEN

When they entered the tent, the first thing Clint noticed was the scent. There were clothes draped everywhere and a lot of colorful scarves. Cory's smell was all around them, and he found that he had an erection. The woman had affected him immediately, and he could only hope that the same was true of her.

Suddenly he felt guilty thinking about sex when Lenny was in such trouble.

"Let's find someplace to sit," Bat said. He looked around and found a trunk to perch himself on.

"Never been in here before, Bat?"

"Nope."

Bat didn't elaborate, but Clint believed him. Oddly, he was glad that his friend had never been inside Cory's tent before.

Of the women in Clint's life, it seemed that there were more redheads among those he remembered most fondly— Joanna Morgan, Lacy Blake, Anne Archer—they were all redheads. Ellie Lennox, in Denver, was dark-haired, but the others had red hair—red like Cory Evers's.

"Lenny," Bat said, drawing Clint back to the business at hand, "tell me where you were last night."

"I told you, I went for a walk."

"Where?"

"Around."

"In town?" Clint asked.

"I don't understand this," Lenny said. "Why do they think I killed someone?"

"Not just someone, Lenny," Clint said. "Remember the woman from the saloon last night? Liz?"

"Is it her who was killed?"

"That's right," Bat said.

"Why do they think I did it?"

"Well, among other things," Bat said, "there's a roomful of people who heard you calling her names. 'Harlot' and . . . what was the other one, Clint?"

"I think it was 'servant of Satan.' "

"There's also the fact that you threw her off your lap," Bat said.

"But . . . but I wouldn't kill her. I wouldn't kill anyone."

"Clint was at the saloon this morning, and he heard them saying that a man was seen near there last night—a man who was about six and a half feet tall. That ring any bells with you, Lenny?"

Suddenly Lenny smiled, and it shocked both Clint and Bat.

"What are you smiling about, boy?" Bat demanded.

"We got nothing to worry about, Bat."

"And why not?"

"Because," Lenny Younger said, his smile growing even wider, "I'm six foot eight."

Clint and Bat looked at each other, and then Bat closed his eyes and shook his head.

"Lenny," Bat said, "let's see if we can't get you to understand this. . . ."

• • •

After talking for twenty minutes straight, Clint and Bat thought that they had gotten Lenny Younger to the point where he understood the problem. At that point Cory Evers returned, with Pop Hingle in tow.

Pop Hingle was about sixty years old, a tall, slender man wearing a dark tuxedo jacket, dark pants, and a high hat—a hat like Clint had seen people wear to the opera in San Francisco.

"Bat," he said, by way of a greeting. "The sheriff's here with some men. They're going to start searching tents in a little while. I could object."

"I understand," Bat said. "Pop, this is my friend, Clint Adams."

"Mr. Adams," Pop said, nodding. "I've heard of you." Nothing else; just that he'd heard of him. No nervousness, no kowtowing, no dirty looks. Clint liked the man right away.

"Lenny, you in trouble?" Pop asked Lenny.

"It looks like it, Pop," Lenny said. "But I didn't do nothing."

"If you say so, I believe you, boy," Pop said. He looked at Clint and Bat and said, "I don't think this boy is capable of telling a lie."

"Neither do I," Cory said.

"If we all agree on that," Clint said, "then we'd better figure out if there are any other six and a half foot—or more—men in the area."

"There was one yesterday," Bat said. "He wrestled Lenny. He was almost as tall as Lenny."

"I beat him," Lenny said.

"What was his name, Bat?"

"Damned if I know," Bat said. "We don't ask anybody's name. That is, unless they beat Lenny."

"Nobody's ever beat me," Lenny said. He was speaking with his head down, with no inflection in his tone.

"No," Bat said, "nobody has."

"Well," Clint said, "I think we'd better go out and find that feller."

"Right," Bat said, "right."

He looked at Clint, and Clint thought he knew what was on Bat's mind.

If Lenny Younger was innocent, then why had he asked for his share of the money, and why was he intent on going back home?

FOURTEEN

They could hear the sounds from outside, which indicated that the search had begun.

"I've instructed my people to make things as unpleasant for the sheriff as possible," Pop Hingle said.

"I don't want you people getting into trouble over this, Pop," Bat said.

"Nothing violent will occur," Pop said. "They'll just bellyache when they're asked to vacate their tents for a search, and they'll move along as slowly as possible. We'll slow them down, don't worry."

"That's good enough," Clint said. "Now all we need is someplace to hide Lenny."

"Why do I have to hide?" Lenny asked. "I didn't do anything."

Lenny's simple mind had come up with the perfect question. Indeed, if he were innocent, why should he have to hide?

"Unfortunately, Lenny," Clint explained, "there are a lot of people who don't believe that you're innocent. You could give yourself up to the sheriff and he'd put you in jail, and we'd have to wait for a judge to arrive before a trial could begin. But somehow I don't think these people would want you to get to trial."

"Especially the sonofabitch who did kill Liz," Bat said.

"I don't understand," Pop said.

"Obviously, someone did kill the woman," Bat said, "and it was either someone Lenny's size or someone who wants everyone to believe that it was Lenny."

"Was there a witness?" Pop asked.

"There was a man who said he saw a big man near the saloon," Clint said. "Bat, since you saw this feller that Lenny wrestled yesterday, I'd suggest you start looking for him."

"And you?"

"I'm going to find the witness and find out if he saw what he says he saw."

"What about Lenny?" Pop asked.

"I have an idea," Cory said.

"Will it work?" Bat asked.

"You tell me," she said, and explained her plan to them.

She intended to move Lenny around from tent to tent, with the help of the other members of their troupe, always leaving him in the tent that had most recently been searched.

"Even if they go back and search again, it will work," she said.

"You sound like you've done this sort of thing before," Clint said.

She gave Clint a dazzling smile and said, "Well, an outfit like this has one or two run-ins with the law, right, Pop?"

"Oh, once in a while," Pop said. "Cory's right, it will work."

"Even with someone Lenny's size?" Bat asked.

"Don't worry," Cory said. "We know many forms of misdirection. We'll make sure that the sheriff and his men are always looking elsewhere."

"How can you be sure of that?" Lenny asked.

"Well," Cory said, smiling, "if I have to I can always take off my top."

Clint found himself wishing he could stay around for that one.

Clint and Bat left first, walking together.

"We'd better not walk through the camp," Clint said. "Somebody's bound to have recognized you when we were shooting at them."

"What makes you say that?"

"Is there anyone else in town who dresses the way you do?"

"What's wrong with the way I dress?" Bat asked.

"Nothing," Clint said. "Let's just say you can be recognized a mile off."

Bat frowned, then reached up, removed his bowler, looked at it with regret, and flipped it back into the tent behind him.

"That'll help," Clint said. "Come on, we'll circle the grounds to get to town. The sheriff and his men should be here for a while."

"My head is cold," Bat said.

"Hey!" Clint called out to a man passing by. He was dressed in brightly colored clothes, and it was fairly obvious that he worked for the fair or carnival.

"Can I do something for ya?" the man asked.

"Can I borrow your hat?" Clint asked.

The man stared at Clint strangely, then shrugged and gave him the hat. It was a beat-up fedora. Clint took the hat, thanked the man, and handed it to Bat. Bat stared at the hat dubiously, then placed it gently atop his head, as if he were afraid it would bite him.

"A perfect fit," Clint said, "and the disguise is complete. Come on, let's get going."

FIFTEEN

Clint and Bat circled the grounds and entered town together. Once in town they split up, agreeing to meet back at Cory's tent.

Clint had the advantage over Bat in his search. Bat had a man's face and figure in his mind, but Clint knew the name of the man he was looking for.

Sam Warner.

He didn't know what Warner did for a living, but he knew his name and what he looked like. All he had to do was ask someone where the man lived or worked. He couldn't ask just anyone, though. Someone was sure to recognize him as the man who was with Bat that morning, one of the men who'd stolen Lenny Younger from the mob.

There was only one person he could think of to ask, and that was Louisa—Louisa, whose last name he didn't even know.

He went to her cafe and found it open, doing a moderate late breakfast business. He took a table so as not to attract too much attention.

"Late breakfast?" she asked.

"I wish I had time," he said. "Do you know a man named Sam Warner?"

"Sam? Of course I know him. He owns and runs the general store."

"The general store. Thank you."

"What's this about?"

He started to get up, then stopped. He should tell her, so that she wouldn't mention to anyone that she had seen him.

"There was a murder last night."

"What?"

"You haven't heard?"

"No," she said, sitting down opposite him. "No, I got up late and came straight down here to open. Nobody's mentioned it."

"Maybe it hasn't gotten around town yet," he said. Then he went on to explain who was killed and how he was involved.

"Are you sure this boy, Lenny, didn't do it?"

Clint rubbed his hand over his jaw.

"I can't be absolutely sure," Clint said, "but I've learned to trust my instincts about people, Louisa. I don't think this boy could kill anyone, let alone a woman."

"So what are you going to do?"

"I guess I'll have to try and find out who did kill the woman."

"Why you? You didn't even know the boy until yesterday."

"I've known Bat Masterson for a long time," Clint said. "I'm doing this to help him, and to help the boy."

"You like doing that, don't you?" she asked. "You like helping people?"

"When they want my help. When they need it."

"Like I do?" she asked, reaching out and touching his hand.

"That was different," he said. "I wanted that, too."

"And do you still want it?"

He thought of Cory Evers, and he spoke the truth.

"I don't know, Louisa."

"Well," she said, smiling, "when you do know, come back and let me know."

"All right," he said. "I'll do that."

"I hope everything turns out all right for you and your friends."

"It would help me if you didn't tell anyone you saw me today."

"Sure," she said. "It's the least I can do."

He nodded his thanks to her, then rose and left the cafe. Now he knew where to find Sam Warner, and he headed right for him.

Bat made a circuit around town first, just to see if he could spot the man. When he didn't, he wasn't quite sure what to do next. He could start asking around, but what would he be asking for? A big man who stood almost six foot six? Chances were that some of the people he asked would point him toward his own wrestler.

A man that size, he wondered, where would he work? The livery? He had never seen him there, but he'd only been to the livery once. He'd try there first. Maybe the man was a blacksmith. Maybe he had his own shop somewhere. He'd do that next: ask around for a blacksmith.

Where else, though? Where to look after that?

He didn't know. He wasn't a damned detective. Clint wasn't, either, but he was better at it than Bat was.

Bat decided to check those two places and then go back and see Clint. Maybe he'd have some answers from his man, or maybe he'd have some ideas. Clint would certainly be able to move around town more freely than Bat would, wouldn't he?

Maybe the best thing to do would be to go and talk to the sheriff. He could do that without telling him where Lenny was.

Bat was at the southern end of town, and he started walking north, heading for the livery stable.

Shit, he thought, playing poker was easier than this. Maybe he should stick to what he knew best from now on and stay out of trouble.

Lenny's mother would probably *never* forgive him for this.

SIXTEEN

Clint stepped into the general store and waited for the man behind the counter to finish with a customer. He was content to wait, because he recognized the man as the same man who had been standing next to him earlier.

Sam Warner.

When the customer turned to leave, Clint closed the door behind the man.

"Excuse me," Sam Warner said good-naturedly. "If we don't leave the door open, my customers might think I'm closed. We wouldn't want that, would we?"

"Actually," Clint said, "for the next five minutes I think we would."

"What?" Warner said. His good nature was quickly replaced by something else: fear. "If you intend to rob me, I have to tell you—"

"I'm not here to rob you, Mr. Warner," Clint said. "I'm just here to talk. I only closed the door so we wouldn't be interrupted."

"Talk?" Warner asked, frowning. "What about?"

"About this morning," Clint said. "And last night."

"I don't understand."

"Don't you remember me?" Clint asked.

"I'm afraid I don't."

"I was standing next to you this morning, in front of the saloon."

Warner frowned, then said, "I think I remember, but I still don't understand."

"Mr. Warner," Clint said, interrupting him, "your description of the man you saw last night has led to suspicion being cast on a friend of mine."

"I see," Warner said. "What would you like me to do? Change my description?"

"Only if what you said wasn't true."

"But it was."

"Well, then, I don't expect you to change it," Clint said. "Maybe you can add to it, though."

"In what way?"

"What else did you notice about the big man you saw?" Clint asked.

Warner thought a moment, then shrugged and said, "Nothing, I'm afraid. I told Sheriff Birch everything I saw."

"And there's nothing you can add?"

"No."

"Forgive me, Mr. Warner, but were you put up to this by someone?"

"Put up to—do you mean, am I lying?"

"That's exactly what I mean."

Warner had gotten over his initial fear, and now he was feeling anger.

"I beg your pardon, Mr.—"

"Adams. Clint Adams."

"Mr. Adams . . . Adams?"

"That's right."

"C-Clint Adams?"

Clint frowned and said, "Yes."

"The Gunsmith?"

"Can we forget about that and get back to the matter at hand, Mr. Warner?"

But Warner's entire attitude had changed now. The anger had drained away, as if someone had pulled a plug in the bottom of his foot. Once again the fear was back, but now he wasn't afraid of a man, he was afraid of a reputation.

"W-what would you like me to say?" Warner asked.

Clint hoped this wouldn't be a waste of time now. The man was so afraid of him now that he might say anything, just to try and satisfy him.

Clint moved closer to the counter to make his point, and Warner took as many steps back as he could before he bumped into a set of shelves.

"Mr. Warner, I don't want you to say anything you don't want to say. All I'm asking you to do is search your memory of last night and see if you can come up with anything else."

"T-that's all?"

"That's all."

"And if I can't come up with anything?"

"I'll leave," Clint said. "All I ask is that you try."

Warner licked his lips and said, "A-all right, I'll try."

"Thank you."

To his credit, the man genuinely seemed to be searching his memory. He closed his eyes, then flicked at a drop of sweat with his forefinger, sending it flying from his nose onto the counter. It was so quiet that Clint actually heard the drop strike the wood.

"I can't . . ." Warner started to say, and then suddenly he opened his eyes and said, "Wait a minute."

"What?"

"There is something," Warner said. "Yes, I remember now. The man was limping."

"The big man?" Clint asked.

"Yes."

"He was hurt?"

"Well, he was limping as he ran away."

"He *ran* away? He didn't walk fast or trot?"

"Well, it was faster than a trot, but he couldn't really run because he was limping." Warner looked at Clint hopefully and asked, "Does that help?"

"Mr. Warner," Clint said, "that could help quite a bit. I thank you."

"Uh, s-should I tell the sheriff what I remembered?"

"Yes, you should," Clint said. "All I ask is that you don't mention me."

"You want me to lie?"

"No, I don't want you to lie," Clint said. "Just don't mention me unless the sheriff specifically asks about me or about how you came to remember the limp. That's not a lie . . . not really. . . . Is it?"

"Well . . . no, I suppose not."

"I'll leave you to your business now, Mr. Warner. Thanks again."

"S-sure."

Clint left the general store, passing a customer as he did so. There was no way of knowing what Warner would tell the sheriff, but whatever he decided to tell the man he would first have to find him, and Sheriff Birch was probably still searching through tents.

Bat found nothing at the livery, and Joshua—who did ask Bat if he had seen Clint that afternoon—told him that *he* was the only blacksmith in town.

"If you see that Adams feller, tell him I got us some more business, will you?"

Joshua had obviously not heard that the sheriff was looking for Bat and for Clint—that is, if anyone had been able to identify Clint to the lawman.

"I'll tell him," Bat promised, and he left.

It was time to go back to Cory's tent. He wasn't quite sure what his next move should be, and maybe Clint was back by now.

SEVENTEEN

As Clint approached the fairgrounds, he saw the sheriff and a couple of his men leaving the grounds. He quickly sought refuge behind a stand of brush until they went by. He gave them time to get far enough away, then came out and walked to Cory's tent. Cory Evers was at the entrance, as if she were waiting for him.

"Glad you're back," he said.

"Me too."

"Bat's inside, with Lenny and Pop."

"How'd the search go?"

"Just like I planned. Did you expect anything less?"

"No," he said, "of course not."

"As you get to know me better, Clint, you'll find that I usually get what I want."

"I'll take that as a warning. Let's go inside."

As he moved to enter, she didn't move, forcing him to brush by her. As they made contact she leaned into him, pressing her breasts against him for a moment.

Inside he found Bat, Lenny, and Pop Hingle sitting together, talking.

"Bat?"

"I couldn't find him, Clint," Bat said. "And asking around was out of the question. I didn't want to call attention to myself."

"I know what you mean."

"What did you find out?"

"Something that can help us, I think," Clint said. "Lenny, how are you doing?"

Lenny had been staring at the floor. Now he looked up at Clint and said, "I don't like hiding. It ain't honest."

"Don't worry about it, Lenny. Everything will turn out all right."

"My mother's not going to like this."

"She'll blame me, Lenny, not you," Bat said. He looked at Clint and asked, "What did you find out?"

"The man Sam Warner saw running from the saloon was limping."

Bat smiled and said, "Lenny's not limping."

Clint didn't bother saying that Lenny could have been limping last night and not this morning.

"No, he's not."

"You know," Bat said, "that feller that Lenny beat yesterday, he went down pretty hard, and I think he was limping when he left."

"That makes it all the more important, that we find him," Clint said. "Pop, can you ask around of your people and see if any of them knows who the man was?"

"I'll start right away," Pop said, moving toward the entrance of the tent. "Cory?"

"I'm going to stay here awhile, Pop."

"Bat, Clint," Pop said, "I'm going to have to get my shows started."

"That's a good idea, Pop," Clint said. "Up to now you can claim that the sheriff kept you from getting started. If you don't start the shows now, they'll know that something is wrong."

"I'll get my people started and question them at the same time."

"Good," Clint said.

When Pop was gone, Cory took his seat. Clint remained standing.

"I want to turn myself in," Lenny said suddenly.

"Uh, Lenny," Bat said, "that's not a good idea."

"Why not?"

"Because everyone in this town is going to think you're guilty."

"But I'm not."

"Believe me," Bat started to say, but he stopped when Lenny stood up.

"I want to turn myself in," Lenny said. "I'm not guilty, and God won't let them hang me."

"God won't let them . . ." Bat said, and he gave Clint a helpless look.

"If he wants to turn himself in, Bat, that's really up to him. He can put his faith in God, but that doesn't mean we can't be trying to help him."

Bat stared at Clint, then looked up at Lenny.

"All right, Lenny," Bat said. "If you want to turn yourself in, I'll go with you."

"This is the right thing to do, Bat," Lenny said.

"Sure, Lenny, sure it is." Bat looked at Clint and said, "Why don't you wait here for me, Clint."

"If you come back," Clint said. "The sheriff might lock you up, too."

"If he does, that means he'll be looking for you. One of us has to stay on the outside to find the real killer. I think you're the best man for that job."

"I'll do my best, Bat."

"Bat," Lenny said, "I can go alone."

"No way, Lenny," Bat said. "We're in this together. Okay?"

Lenny smiled for the first time that day and said, "Okay, Bat."

Bat and Lenny left, leaving Clint and Cory alone.

"He's so young and so trusting," Cory said.

"I know," Clint said. "I don't know if I was ever that young *or* that trusting."

"What will you do now?"

"I'll give Bat an hour and see if he comes back. After that, I'll have to start looking again."

"Do you want some coffee?"

"Sure."

"I'll be right back with it."

"Thanks."

Cory started to leave, then turned and said, "Clint, whatever happens, I'll be helping you."

"I don't want you to get in trouble with the law, Cory."

She laughed and said, "Believe me, mister, it wouldn't be the first time."

Clint watched her leave, then laughed softly to himself. It probably wouldn't be the last time, either.

EIGHTEEN

Cory brought Clint a cup of coffee and one for herself and sat down next to him.

"The shows are in full swing," she told him, "all except Bat's Oregon Strangler."

"Poor choice of name, as it turns out," Clint said. "What about you?"

"Me?" she repeated.

"Yes, don't you have to dance? I wouldn't want you to get fired."

She seemed to find the idea of getting fired very funny.

"I dance when I want to," she said. "With no danger of getting fired when I don't."

"Why is that?"

"Because I'm the top attraction," she said. "Also, Pop Hingle is my uncle."

"Well, that sure helps."

"It can't hurt."

They drank their coffee and then set the empty cups aside.

"Still have about forty minutes," she said.

"You're right," Clint said. "Maybe I should walk around some."

"That wasn't what I had in mind."

She stood up, walked to the tent entrance, and released the flap. The tent instantly grew darker, but not so dark that he couldn't see the look in her eyes as she turned and walked toward him.

She surprised him by sliding gently into his lap. He was surprised at how light she was. He could feel the heat of her flesh through the gauzy fabric of her costume. She could feel his reaction to her swelling beneath her.

She licked her lips and asked, "You don't mind?"

"Not at all," he said, sliding his arms around her. "I've been thinking about this since we first met earlier today."

She licked her lips again and then pressed them to his. They were wet and warm, and her tongue was like silk as it snaked into his mouth. She moaned as his tongue moved over hers and as his hands moved over her body. He cupped one breast through the scarves she wore, and she laughed and moved her mouth away from his.

"Pull," she said.

"Where?"

"Here." She showed him the end to pull. As he tugged it, a scarf fell away. "And here." Another tug, another scarf. "Here," she said, "and here . . . and here . . ."

Two full breasts blossomed into his hands, the nipples hard against his palms.

She lifted herself in his lap and he helped her slide off the silk panties she wore. She unbuttoned his shirt and began kissing his chest, running her tongue over his nipples. His erection, pinned between them, felt as if it would explode at any moment. His heart was beating very quickly. He knew it was because of the girl, but also because of the situation.

He slid his arms beneath her, took her weight, and stood up.

"Where?" he asked.

"There." She pointed.

He hadn't seen it before, but there was a bed of pillows in a corner of the tent. He walked to it and deposited her gently upon it. While she watched, he undressed, wondering what he would do if someone entered just then: Pop Hingle or even Bat.

"Come to me, Clint," she said, holding her arms out to him. Her breasts lifted with the movement, the nipples tight and hard.

He did as she asked. He slid into her embrace, her flesh burning him, in more ways than one.

He explored her body with his tongue and his mouth, tasting her sweetness and her tartness, and then he pierced her tartness, driving himself right to the core of her.

"Oh, God . . ." she moaned, lifting her hips to meet his thrusts. "Yes, oh, yesssss . . ."

They moved together, both grunting with the effort. He tried to support his weight with a hand on each side of her, but the pillows kept moving. She solved his problem by putting her arms around him and pulling his weight down on top of her.

"I won't break," she whispered. "I promise. . . ."

And she didn't. Finally, she exploded beneath him, writhing, sliding, even kicking as he tried to stay with her, and then finally he came as well, and she bit her lip to keep from screaming.

NINETEEN

"He didn't do it, Sheriff," Bat said.

"A judge will decide that, Masterson." Birch looked at Lenny and said, "Let's go, son."

As Lenny started for the cells in the back, Birch looked at Bat and said, "Don't go anywhere, Masterson. I still haven't decided whether or not to arrest you yet."

"Don't press your luck," Bat said.

Birch cleared his throat and took Lenny into the back. Bat heard the cell door shut, and then Birch returned.

"You were smart to bring him in."

"I didn't bring him," Bat said. "He brought me."

"What?"

"It was his idea to give himself up."

"Then he confessed?"

"I told you, he didn't do it. Of course he didn't confess."

"Well, we'll convict him then."

"Not without a witness."

"We have a witness."

"Bring him in and let him identify him."

"I . . . don't think I need you to tell me how to do my job, Masterson."

"*Mr.* Masterson."

83

Birch averted his eyes from Bat's steely stare and said, "Mr. Masterson."

"Somebody ought to tell how to do your job, Sheriff," Bat said, "because you don't know what the hell you're doing."

"Mast—*Mr. Masterson*, the boy came in and gave himself up. What am I supposed to do, let him go?"

"He didn't do it, and you can't prove that he did."

"I have to let the judge decide that."

"Does this one-horse town have a judge?"

"No," Birch said. "I'll have to send for a circuit judge."

"That'll take a week, easy; maybe more."

"Sure."

"All right," Bat said, "that gives me and Clint time to find the real killer."

"Clint?"

"Clint Adams."

"Adams?" Birch asked. "You mean the Gunsmith?"

"That's right."

"He's the other man who was with you this morning?"

"Right again."

Bat noticed that Birch's hands had begun to shake a bit. Obviously, the sheriff wasn't prepared to handle a situation that involved both Bat Masterson and Clint Adams.

"Sheriff, maybe you'd be smart to send for a federal lawman. It might not take as long as getting a judge, and maybe he'll be smart enough to cut Lenny free."

"I'll . . . I'll think about it."

"Good," Bat said. "That's the first smart thing I've heard you say."

Bat turned and walked over to the doorway that led to the cells.

"Lenny, just relax. We'll have you out in no time."

"I'm gonna say some prayers, Bat."

Bat closed his eyes, then opened them and said, "You do that, kid."

Clint and Cory dressed afterward. This time she put on more conventional clothing—a shirt and a skirt. She was pulling on her boots when Bat called from outside.

"Come on in, Bat."

When Bat entered they were sitting as they had been when they were drinking coffee. Bat looked at them both, but if he noticed anything he kept his mouth shut.

"How'd it go?" Clint asked.

"The sheriff is a moron," Bat replied. "But at least he didn't lock me up."

"Is there a judge in this town?" Clint asked.

"No, he's sending for a circuit judge. I tried to get him to send for some federal law."

"You think he'll do it?"

"I don't know."

"A circuit judge—that'll take the better part of a week, maybe more." Clint turned to Cory and asked, "How much longer will you and your people be here?"

She shrugged.

"Depends on how well we're doing," she said. "I'll have to ask Pop."

"Why don't you do that for me, honey," Clint said.

"Sure," she said, standing up. "I'll take care of it right now."

Both men watched her leave, and then Bat looked over at the disheveled pillows.

"I have been trying—"

"Never mind," Clint said.

"Not going to kiss and tell, huh?"

"I never do."

"Really?" Bat said. "No wonder she's always watching me."

Bat sat down where Cory had been sitting. "All right," he said, "what do we do now?"

"Let's wait and see what Pop Hingle finds out from his people." Clint looked around the interior of the tent and said, "At least we won't have to hide in here anymore. . . . Will we?"

"No," Bat said. "The sheriff isn't man enough to try and lock either one of us up."

"What about the townspeople?"

Bat laughed and said, "You saw them scatter this morning."

"Lenny's sitting in a cell," Clint said. "Do you think Birch would stand up to a lynch mob?"

"Not a chance."

"One of us had better be within shouting distance of the jail at all times," Clint said. "Meanwhile, since we're not hiding, we can ask around town for the man who wrestled Lenny yesterday."

Bat stood up.

"I'll get started on that now, while you wait for Pop . . . and for Cory."

Bat started to leave, then turned and said, "You might want to straighten out those pillows before Pop gets here—you lucky dog."

Bat left, then came back in. He looked around, found what he was looking for, picked up his bowler, and put it back on.

He looked at Clint and said, "Now he can start watching *you* like a hawk."

TWENTY

Clint waited in Cory's tent, and she soon returned with Pop Hingle in tow.

"Pop," Clint said, standing up. Inadvertently, he looked over at the pillows, which he had tried to arrange in some semblance of order. The problem was, there *was* no order for the pillows. They simply tumbled over one another. He only hoped it didn't look like they had been recently used.

"Clint," Pop said, "I talked to all my people. I'm afraid none of them seem to know who the man was who wrestled Lenny."

"Well, it was worth a try, Pop," Clint said. "Bat's out trying to spot the man now. I guess I'll go on out and help him."

"Wait a minute," Pop said. "Before you go, we may have something for you."

"Like what?"

"Well, one of my people said that after Lenny had beaten the man, he limped off with two other men."

"And?"

"And he thinks he knows who one of the men was."

"Who?"

"A feller they call Georgie, he said," Pop replied.

"Does he know where I can find Georgie?"

Pop made a face and shook his head.

"No, he doesn't. He just said that he saw him around for several days and that he had heard some people call him Georgie."

"Does he know if this Georgie is a local, or was he passing through?"

"I asked him that. He said he got the impression that he was local."

Clint lifted his hands away from his sides and then let them fall back, slapping his thighs.

"All right then. Now we have to find Georgie."

"Would you like me to give you some people to help you search?"

"No," Clint said, holding a hand up. "I don't want to take any of your people away from you. You've got a fair to run." Clint frowned and asked, "Or is it a carnival?"

"It depends," Pop said, smiling. "Some towns worry when they hear that a carnival is coming to town. Carnies have somehow gotten bad reputations."

"Carnies?"

"Anyone who works or travels with a carnival is a carny," Cory explained.

"Bad reputations as what?"

"Name it," Cory said. "Thieves, baby snatchers, rustlers, anything people want to blame on us.

"When we got to Oregon and found out we'd be playing a succession of small towns, we decided to call our outfit a fair. It seems to have worked so far."

"Well, I hope it keeps working," Clint said. He started to leave, and then said, "Oh yeah, one more thing: Cory says that whether or not you stay on here will depend on how much money you're making."

"Not necessarily."

"Oh?"

"Until he tells me different," Pop said, "Lenny is one of my people, and when one of my people is in jail I don't desert him. We'll be around until you clear him . . . or prove he did it."

"Well, I don't think he did it, so we'll just go on trying to clear him," Pop said. "I'm sure Lenny will appreciate this, Pop."

"He's a nice kid," Pop said. "I hope he'll stay on with us, even when Bat leaves."

Clint didn't bother to tell Pop that Lenny and Bat had been on their way to the bank to get Lenny's money so that he could go back home. He decided to hold that back until later.

"I'd better get going."

"I'll come with you and help you look," Cory said, moving to his side and standing with her hands clasped behind her back.

"Maybe you'd better stay here," Clint said, looking at Pop Hingle.

The older man shrugged and said, "I've given up trying to tell her what to do, Clint. She has a mind of her own, like her mother—my sister—may she rest in peace."

"Cory—"

"Clint, you need me with you on this."

"Why?"

"Because," she said with a smile, "I know what this feller Georgie looks like."

"Well, why didn't you say so in the first place?" Clint said. "Come on, let's get started."

When they got outside and headed back to town Clint asked, "What do you know about Georgie?"

"Only that I've seen him around," Cory said. "He never seems to have any money, yet people seem to buy him things—mostly food and drinks."

"Is he a drunk?" If he was, that would make him easy to find. They wouldn't have to look any farther than the saloon.

"I don't think so," she said, shaking her head. Her shoulder-length hair swayed with the movement. "I just think he's homeless and jobless."

"Well, he may not be the town drunk then," Clint said, "but the saloon is still a good place to start." He looked at her and asked, "Have you ever been in a saloon?"

"I was dancing in saloons when I was fourteen," she said, laughing. Clint had a feeling that the laughter was a bit forced.

Clint decided that this young woman had probably led a very hard, yet very interesting, life. He wouldn't have minded hearing more about it, but that would have to wait until later.

TWENTY-ONE

Clint and Cory went to the saloon, which was doing a brisk business. Clint suspected that the reason for the good business this early in the evening was probably the murder. The killing of a woman had to be the topic of conversation on most people's minds, and the best place to discuss it would be the saloon.

As they entered, the conversation in the place fell off abruptly. Clint knew that it had nothing to do with him, but it did have a lot to do with the woman who was at his side. He felt an odd surge of pride that everyone had seen Cory enter with him.

He walked to the bar with Cory keeping pace.

The bartender was wiping his hands on a rag, watching Clint carefully.

"Beer," Clint said.

"For the lady, too?"

Clint hesitated, but Cory said, "Of course."

The bartender went off to get the two beers and Clint looked at Cory.

"Beer?"

"A bad habit I picked up in my youth. Remember?"

"Yes," Clint said, "you were dancing in places like this when you were fourteen."

"Right."

"What other bad habits did you pick up?"

She did something with her eyebrows and said, "That's for you to find out."

The bartender returned and set the beers in front of them. Clint dropped some coins on the bar.

"Thanks."

"Sure."

"Before you go," Clint said, "I'm looking for Georgie."

"So?"

This was the same bartender who had been friendly to him yesterday. There was no trace of that friendly attitude today. Clint guessed that he had been tied in with Bat and Lenny. Since Lenny was suspected of the murder, Bat would probably get the same treatment the next time he came in as well.

"Can you tell me where to find him?"

"That's kind of hard to say," the man said.

"Why?" Clint asked when the man did not continue.

"He doesn't live anywhere," the bartender said. "He just sort of sleeps wherever he can find a spot."

"Where does he eat?"

"Same thing," the man said. "He eats and drinks where he can."

"Here?"

The man shrugged. "Sometimes."

"Is he the town drunk?"

"Georgie's no drunk," the bartender said. "He's just had some bad breaks."

"I see."

Clint decided to check the cafe next. Maybe Louisa was in the habit of feeding Georgie.

"Thanks for the beer."

"Don't thank me," the bartender said. "You paid for it."

Clint turned to leave and found his way blocked by three fair-sized men. None of them, however, was six and a half feet tall. That would have been too easy.

They were all big, though—six feet or better—and well fed. And they were all armed.

"What do you want with Georgie, friend?" one of them asked.

"I just want to ask him some questions."

"About what?"

"That's between him and me, isn't it?"

The spokesman looked at the other two men, and then said to Clint, "Well, maybe we're making it our business, too."

"I don't think so," Clint said. "Excuse us."

Clint and Cory went forward, but the men did not move. In fact, one of them used an elbow to shove Cory back a few steps. She retaliated by kicking him in the shin.

"Jesus!" the man roared. Then he said, "Cunt!" and grabbed for Cory.

Clint moved quickly, grabbing the man's arm and twisting it around, then bringing his own elbow down on his captors. The man's arm bent the wrong the way, and he screamed. Clint released him, and the man went down to one knee, cradling his arm.

"Apologize to the lady," Clint said to him.

"Jesus," one of the others said, staring at Clint.

"Apologize," Clint said again.

The fallen man looked up at Cory and said from behind clenched teeth, "S-sorry."

Clint looked at the spokesman and said, "Stand aside . . . please."

"Y-you broke his arm," the man stammered.

"I doubt it," Clint said. "It's probably just sprained. He'll be fine, but if you've got a doctor I'd take your friend to see him."

"There was no call for that," the spokesman said. "We was just talking."

"Friend," Clint said calmly, "I'm through talking. Are you going to move aside and let us pass?"

"Sure," the man said. "Sure, mister." He looked at Cory and added, "Sorry, miss."

As Clint and Cory walked to the door, the two men helped the third man to his feet.

Outside, Cory said, "Wow!"

Clint looked at her and asked, "You still want to tag along?"

"I wouldn't miss it," she said. "This promises to be more fun than I've had in a long time."

TWENTY-TWO

There were some people having an early dinner at Louisa's. As during the other times Clint had been there, Louisa was working alone.

"We'd better take a table," Clint said.

Louisa looked over at Clint and started to smile. The smile slipped when she saw Cory with him.

"Do you know her?" Cory asked.

"Yes."

"That explains why I'm getting dirty looks."

"You're imagining it."

"Sure," Cory said, smiling at him. "Sure I am. You and women, you get along, don't you?"

Clint grinned and said, "I get along with everyone."

"We are about to put that statement to the test," Cory said. Clint looked up and saw Louisa walking over.

"Hello, Louisa."

"Hello, Clint," she said. She looked at Cory. "Who is your friend?"

"This is Cory Evers. She's with the carn—the fair."

"Ah, how interesting," Louisa said, looking anything but interested. "Maybe I get you both something?"

"Some information," Clint said.

Louisa frowned. "About what?"

95

"A man called Georgie."

Louisa folded her arms in front of her and asked, "What do you want with Georgie?"

"I want to ask him some questions."

"Georgie? What could you want to ask him about?"

"The murder."

"Georgie?" she said, again. "He's the most harmless man I know."

"Do you know where I could find him?"

She thought a moment, then said, "There's never any way to tell where he'll be."

"Does he ever come here?"

"Sometimes," she said. "Sometimes I feed him."

"Today?"

"No, not today."

"Then he still might show up."

"I guess."

She seemed reticent to talk about Georgie, like the bartender.

"What is it about Georgie that makes everyone want to protect him?"

"I told you," Louisa said. "He's harmless."

"A drunk?"

"No," she said. "He was once, but not anymore."

"Is he . . . disabled in any way?"

"What do you mean?"

"I mean is he physically or mentally—"

"He's fine."

"Why doesn't he work?"

"He does, sometimes."

"Doing what?"

"Cleaning."

"Cleaning what?"

"Whatever needs to be cleaned," Louisa said. "My

floor, the saloon floor, the livery—" She stopped short when she said *livery*, as if she might have said too much.

"The livery?"

She looked away and said, "Sometimes. Look, do you want anything? I've got customers."

"No," Clint said, "not right now, thanks. We'd better go."

"Sure," Louisa said. She gave Cory another look, which Cory returned innocently, and then went off to care for her other customers.

"Louisa?"

"Yes?" she said, turning back.

"If you knew where Georgie was, would you tell me?"

She thought about that for a moment, then said, "I don't know."

"If you see him," Clint said, "tell him it's worth money to him to talk to me."

"I'll tell him . . . if I see him."

Clint rose, motioning for Cory to get up also, and they went outside.

"You sure do get along with everyone," Cory said.

"Why is it that women can't get along with everyone?"

"Like who?"

"Like each other."

"Two women who have slept with the same man," Cory said wisely, "never hit it off. Do two men who have slept with the same woman make fast friends?"

"I don't know," Clint said. "I don't usually share women with friends."

"Wise choice."

"Let's go over to the livery."

TWENTY-THREE

When Clint entered the livery, Joshua almost charged him.

"Clint, Jesus, we got a lot of business!" he said. He was agitated, not wanting to lose the money that would be coming from that business. "Look."

He led Clint back to his rig. Clint looked inside, and it looked like someone was hoarding guns.

"I'll bet you know what's wrong with all of them, don't you?"

"Sure I do," Joshua said. "I, uh, just don't remember which is which . . . exactly."

"I'll get to them later, Joshua," Clint said. "For now, tell me what you know about Georgie."

"Georgie? What do you want with Georgie?"

"I want to ask him some questions. I know he's homeless, I know he used to drink but doesn't anymore, and I know that he occasionally works cleaning up. Does he clean up for you?"

"Sometimes."

"Does he ever sleep here?"

"Sure . . . sometimes."

"Have you seen him lately?"

Joshua frowned.

"I haven't seen him today. I think I saw him yesterday."

"Where?"

"He was on his way to the fair, I think."

"Was there anyone with him?"

Joshua thought about that.

"A big man, maybe?" Clint asked, prompting him. "Almost six and a half feet tall?"

"Not that I can remember," Joshua said. "I think he was going alone."

"Maybe he met some friends there?"

"Georgie ain't got any friends."

"No?" Clint said. "Seems to me the whole town is full of his friends."

"Not personal," Joshua said. "The town sort of takes care of him, but nobody is really personal friends with him."

"Do you know a big man, Joshua? A real big man?"

"Just the one they got in the jail."

"What do you know about him?"

"Everybody says he killed Liz."

"Who's 'everybody'?"

"I don't know," Joshua said, shrugging. "Just everybody."

"I think somebody else killed her, Joshua," Clint said. "I think there's another big man in town, and I think he killed Liz."

Joshua thought again, then shook his head and said, "I don't know a big man who lives in town."

"Outside of town, then?"

Joshua rubbed his jaw.

"Maybe . . ."

"Who?"

"There's a feller who's been in here once or twice," Joshua said. "He brings his horse here when he comes to town. He's kinda big—not as big as the kid in jail, I don't think, but pretty big."

"Does he limp?"

"What? No, I don't think so."

The limp had probably come from wrestling Lenny.

"What's the man's name?"

"I don't know," Joshua said. "He don't come to town often enough for me to know his name."

"And you don't know where he lives?"

Joshua shrugged and said, "Outside of town somewhere."

"And you don't know if Georgie knows the man?"

"How would I know that?"

Clint gave Cory a look that betrayed his impatience and frustration.

"Joshua, do you have a horse that this young lady can ride?"

"Sure."

"Saddle it up, will you? I'll saddle my horse."

Joshua grinned at Clint. "Going for a little ride?"

"Yeah," Clint said, "we're going for a little ride."

TWENTY-FOUR

As Clint and Cory mounted up, Clint suddenly changed his mind.

"Before we ride out," Clint said, "I want to locate Bat."

"Okay," she said. "You're the boss."

"We can split this search," Clint explained. "We'll go north and east, and he can go south and west. If there are any homesteaders in the area, between us we should be able to find them."

"Sounds good to me."

"Let's see where the hell he is. . . ."

Bat was at the jail, talking first to Lenny, then to the sheriff.

"How you doing, boy?"

"Fine," Lenny said. "Nobody is mistreating me, Bat."

"That's good," Bat said. "We'll have you out of here in no time."

"The Lord will have me out."

I don't see the Lord searching this whole town like me and Clint are, Bat thought.

"You and Clint may get me out," Lenny said, as if reading Bat's mind, "but we are all instruments of the Lord, Bat.

My mother taught me that a long time ago, and I still believe it."

"You mean that by wrestling, you believe that you were doing the Lord's work?"

"Of course," Lenny said. "If the Lord didn't want me to wrestle, He wouldn't have made me so good at it."

"And if He didn't want me to be a gambler, He wouldn't have made *me* so good at it?"

"Yes."

"That's a fine belief, boy," Bat said, "but doesn't that mean that you can write off any sin by saying that if the Lord didn't want you to be a sinner, He wouldn't have made you so good at it?"

Lenny opened his mouth to answer, then shut it and frowned.

"You think about that for a while, boy," Bat said. "I'm going to talk to the sheriff."

Bat went into the sheriff's office and found the man seated at his desk.

"Get in touch with the circuit judge?"

"I sent a telegram to Eugene," the man said. "Don't have an answer yet."

"What about a marshal?"

The sheriff nodded and said, "Sent a telegram to Eugene about that, too."

"Maybe you ain't as dumb as I think you are, Sheriff," Bat said.

"Hey," Birch said, half rising, but then he remembered that he was talking to Bat Masterson and sat back down. "That ain't . . . right."

"Maybe not," Bat said, "but any man who would put that boy in jail for murder—for murdering a *woman*—just ain't right in the head."

"The boy confessed!"

"He did not confess," Bat said. "He turned himself in because he knew you were looking for him."

"Why would he turn himself in if he didn't do it?" Birch said. "Tell me that."

"You get on a witness stand and give that as your reason to believe he did it, and the judge will laugh you out of his court. The boy felt it was the right thing to turn himself in. He didn't feel it was right to run and hide if you were looking for him."

Birch stared at Bat and said, "And you think *I'm* not right in the head? What kind of thinking is that?"

"Sheriff," Bat said, "you just never knew anyone as decent as this boy."

"Don't seem so decent to me to be strangling women," Birch muttered.

Bat stared at the sheriff, wanting to grab him, pull him out of his seat, and slap him a few times.

He held himself in check and said instead, "You better make sure that boy gets fed."

"He don't look like he's gonna waste away none," Sheriff Birch said.

"I don't care," Bat said. "You just take good care of him."

"Sure. Sure I will."

"I'll be back later."

Bat went to the door and stepped out onto the boardwalk. As he did, he saw Clint and Cory riding by.

"Hey!" he shouted.

Clint turned his head at the sound of Bat's voice and saw him standing in front of the sheriff's office. He wheeled Duke around and rode over, with Cory close behind.

"How's Lenny?" Clint asked.

"He's fine," Bat said. "He thinks you and I are servants of the Lord."

"Let him think whatever comforts him."

"Where are you two off to?" Bat asked.

Clint explained what they had found out so far about Georgie and about the big man they were looking for.

"All right," Bat said. "I'll get myself a horse and get started."

"We'll meet back at Cory's tent . . . if that's all right with you, Cory."

"Sure," she said. "It's the biggest tent on the grounds."

"Bigger than Pop's?" Clint asked.

"Pop lives in a wagon," she said. Clint decided it wasn't for him to worry about who lived where and who had the bigger tent.

"We'll look as far as we can until it gets dark," Clint said. "That should give us a few hours."

"Agreed," Bat said.

"What's wrong, Bat?" Clint asked. "Something bothering you?"

"Everything," Bat said. "The sheriff's attitude, Lenny's damned attitude. Can you imagine somebody sitting in a cell calmly, waiting for the Lord to break him out?"

"Who are we to say he shouldn't believe it?" Cory asked.

"Nobody," Clint said. "We're nobody. Let's just get him out."

TWENTY-FIVE

Georgie watched the killer wash his hands and torso, then dry himself off.

"Well, what are you gonna do?" Georgie asked.

"About what?"

"About the two men who are looking for you," Georgie said.

"Who are they again?"

"You know who," Georgie said. "Bat Masterson and Clint Adams."

The man turned to face Georgie.

"Very famous men."

"Dangerous men."

"Yes," the killer said, "that, too."

Georgie watched the killer move as he got dressed. He wished he were big and strong. What would he do if he were that big and strong?

"How did he beat you? That Oregon Strangler? How did he beat you?"

The killer frowned. He didn't like thinking about it, let alone talking about it.

"Was he stronger than you?" Georgie asked.

"No."

"Faster?"

"Maybe," the killer said, putting on his shirt.

"But that wasn't it?"

"No."

"Then what?"

The killer turned again and looked at Georgie, his shirt half on and half off.

"He knew things that I didn't," he finally said.

"About what?"

"About wrestling."

"What is there to know?"

"Leverage," the killer said. "Certain holds . . ."

"What is 'leverage'?"

"Leverage is very important," the killer said. "It enables a smaller man to beat a bigger man."

"You mean that with leverage I could beat you?"

"It's possible," the killer said, putting his shirt completely on and buttoning it.

Georgie seemed very excited.

"Could you teach me leverage?"

"If I knew it," the killer said, "that boy wouldn't have beaten me."

"How's your leg?"

The killer looked down at the offending leg, the right one. He had landed on it hard when the boy threw him, and he was still limping.

"It's fine."

"You're still limping," Georgie said. "They're looking for a man with a limp. You might have to stay out of town for a while."

"That's no problem."

"How come you hardly ever go to town?"

"I like being alone."

"What about me?"

"You?"

"Why do you let me come around?"

"I'm using you, Georgie," the killer said. "You go to town for me."

"Only I can't go to town anymore," Georgie said. "They're looking for me, too."

"That's true," the killer said thoughtfully.

"Can I stay here?"

Still thoughtful, the killer said, "I suppose you'll have to, won't you?"

"I guess so," Georgie said happily. "I can sleep on the floor."

When the killer had first met Georgie he'd recognized him right away for what he was. He was more dog than man, looking for someone to feed him, someone to follow; and for a while it had suited the killer to do that for Georgie, while using Georgie for his own purposes.

Now, however, if Georgie couldn't go to town either, then the killer didn't need him anymore, did he?

He didn't have any more need for him.

The killer walked up behind Georgie and put his hands on his shoulders.

"What are you doing?" Georgie asked.

"I'm going to teach you leverage."

"I thought you didn't know any."

"I know enough . . ." the killer said.

He put a hand on either side of Georgie's head, then suddenly twisted it. The sound of the neck cracking was very audible in the quiet room.

"Enough to do this," he said, patting Georgie's dead cheek.

The killer hitched his team to his buckboard, then threw Georgie into the back of it. He drove a few miles from his cabin and dropped Georgie's body off a cliff. He listened as it fell, striking a rock or a precipice here and there, until it finally landed at the bottom.

The killer had come to this region months before, leaving his past behind—or so he'd thought.

Now it was happening all over again.

The saloon girl had been the first, but there would be more. He knew that. He wouldn't be able to help himself.

There was unfinished business, however. Georgie had told him about the man who had seen him, the man who could testify that the killer had been limping that night.

The man's name was Sam Warner.

TWENTY-SIX

Clint and Cory found that there weren't many homesteads in the area. There were a lot of cabins, some inhabited, some uninhabited. The inhabited ones yielded families, mostly squatters who had found the cabins abandoned. Some of them had men living in them, resting until it was time to move on. The land thereabouts was too hard for farming and not healthy enough to raise cattle or horses. There were parts of Oregon that were different, but not here. Here people were living from day to day, unless one were a businessman, living in a town; unless one's business were logging, hauling, or hunting.

They passed several streams, and Clint thought that he could sit on the bank, throw a line into the water, and just sit there and fish—if it weren't so cold.

He looked at Cory and saw that she was shivering. She hadn't dressed warmly enough for riding.

"Here," he said, pulling off his jacket.

"No," she said, but he forced her to put the jacket on. She felt his warmth immediately.

"I've got long underwear," he told her. He didn't tell her that it was back in his hotel room.

They continued on until Clint started to feel the cold. A couple of hours had passed, and he figured it was time to turn back.

They were riding back when he saw the cliff. The ground was hard and wouldn't hold tracks, but the brush in the area had been trampled down, as if a wagon had passed.

"Wait a minute," he said. "Stay here."

He left her there and rode toward the cliff. Short of the edge he dismounted, dropped Duke's reins to the ground, walked to the edge, and looked down.

"What is it?" Cory called out.

Clint hesitated, staring down at the man at the base of the cliff, then turned and picked up Duke's reins. He walked back to where Cory was waiting.

"What is it?" she asked again.

"A body," Clint said, looking down at the ground. "Somebody drove it here in a buckboard or a wagon and threw it over."

"Who is it?"

"I don't know."

"Georgie?"

"Wouldn't that be something!"

"Well, if it is Georgie," Corey asked, "wouldn't that clear Lenny?"

"No," Clint said. "There's no proof that it's connected."

"What are you going to do?" she asked.

"First I'm going to go down and check to see if he's dead."

"He must be."

"I agree," Clint said, "but I'd like to see how he died."

"And after that?"

"We'll go and tell the sheriff. He can have someone come out and pick up the body. When they get to town, someone can identify it."

"And if it is Georgie?"

"Then somebody killed him to keep him quiet," Clint said. "As soon as Bat and I began looking for him, he became a liability."

"But we can't prove that."

"No," Clint said, "but if this is Georgie—"

He stopped short.

"What is it?"

"No sense theorizing until we *know* whether or not it's Georgie. Here," he said, handing her Duke's reins. "I'll be right back."

He left her there and made his way down the face of the cliff. When he reached the man, he stopped and looked down at him. He'd been badly cut up from the fall and lay there like a child's broken doll. His upper half was lying on his back, but his lower half was twisted around. Actually, he wasn't a "he" anymore, but a dead body, to be referred to as "it."

Clint crouched down next to it and looked it over. He examined the man's face. He touched it, pushed it, found that it simply flopped over. The neck was broken cleanly, but there was no significant damage to the face. It was as if the rest of the body had protected the face. Still, if the face had not taken a substantial blow, how had the neck broken? And had it broken before or after the fall? A doctor would know.

The quicker they returned to town, the quicker they'd get the body to town for the doctor to look at. He decided to stop playing detective, so he climbed back up the face of the cliff.

"Well?"

"He's busted up pretty bad," Clint said, mounting up. "And the neck is broken."

"Before or after the fall?" Cory asked.

"I'm not a doctor," Clint said, "but my guess would be before."

"And then he was thrown off the cliff?"

"Again, that's my guess." Clint frowned and looked up at the sky. "It'll be dark in minutes. Let's get back to town and talk to the sheriff."

"Do you think he'll send anyone out here at night?" Corey asked.

"I doubt it. We'll probably have to wait until morning." He looked at her and said, "Come on. We may just make it back before it gets totally dark."

TWENTY-SEVEN

When they got back they first went to Cory's tent to see if Bat was back. He was, having returned half an hour before they had.

"I came up blank," Bat said. "But from the looks on your faces, I'd say you didn't."

"We found a dead man."

"The one we been looking for? With the limp?"

Clint gave Bat a weary look and said, "He's dead. How can we tell if he's got a limp?"

"Oops!" Bat said. "Sorry."

"Never mind," Clint said. "I'm sorry. I'm just tired. The dead man's not big enough to be the one with the limp. I think it's this Georgie we were looking for."

"How do we find out?"

"We'll have to go over and tell the sheriff. He'll have someone go out tomorrow and pick up the body. When they get it back to town, someone will identify it."

"And if it is Georgie," Bat said, "we're back where we started."

"Not necessarily," Clint said. "I'm sure this man was killed first, then dropped off this cliff. His neck's broken, and it had to have been done by a strong man."

"So we've got our man worried."

"I still think he lives out there somewhere, probably in an abandoned shack," Clint said. "We'll have to continue looking tomorrow."

"All right."

"Bright and early."

Bat made a face and said, "If we must, we must."

Clint looked at Cory. "Why don't you settle down and get some rest. I'll go and talk to the sheriff."

"All right," she said, massaging the back of her neck. "I could use a bath."

"Bat, I'll talk to the sheriff," Clint said. "I don't think you and he are on very good terms."

"I wonder whose fault that is?" Bat said. "The man's an idiot."

"I'll keep that in mind."

"Come back and have something to eat," Cory said as Clint headed out of the tent.

He turned, nodded, and said, "I'll be back."

As Clint entered the sheriff's office, he saw that there was a different man behind the desk.

"Can I help ya?" the man asked. He was more boy than man, wearing a deputy's badge and probably no good for much else except watching the office.

"Where's the sheriff?"

"Went out to get some dinner."

"The cafe or the hotel?"

"The cafe," the deputy said. "He likes the food there better."

"Thanks."

"Sure I can't help—" the deputy started to say, but Clint was already out the door.

When he reached the cafe he saw that every table

was taken. There was an empty chair at the sheriff's table however, and he took it.

Birch looked up in surprise as Clint sat down.

"Oh, it's you," the sheriff said.

"Don't let me interrupt your meal," Clint said.

Birch kept staring at Clint nervously, then turned his attention back to the food on his plate. He was having a steak with potatoes, and the juice running from the steak made Clint afraid that he would start drooling any minute.

"I have some news."

"About what?" Birch asked without looking up. He felt as nervous in the presence of the Gunsmith as he did with Bat Masterson.

Clint told him about the body he and Cory had found north of town, and Birch finally raised his eyes again.

"Sandy-haired, no chin, dirty clothes?"

"That sounds right."

"That'd be Georgie, all right," Birch said. "Poor bastard finally walked off the edge of a cliff and done himself in, huh?"

"Are you saying he killed himself?"

"Well, maybe not on purpose . . ."

"Everything I heard about the man tells me he wasn't a drunk."

"Not no more, he wasn't, but he coulda started drinking again and walked off that cliff. I mean, Georgie's life wasn't one anyone would want to trade him for."

"Sheriff," Clint said, leaning forward, "I believe this man was killed. I think his neck was broken first, and then he was thrown from that cliff."

"No way of telling for sure, is there?"

"Yes, there is," Clint said. "Tomorrow we'll go out there and collect the body, then bring it back here so the doctor can have a look at it. Does that sound all right with you?"

"Well . . . sure," Birch said. "Can't leave old Georgie lying out there, can we?"

"No, we can't," Clint said. "Sheriff, I feel certain that the same man who killed Liz also killed Georgie."

"Why?"

"To keep Georgie from telling."

"Why would Georgie know who the killer was? Would the killer have told him? Or let him watch?"

"I don't know," Clint said. "Maybe we'll have to ask the killer that when we catch him. Sheriff, don't you think it's about time you let the boy out of jail?"

"Mr. Adams," Birch said. He stopped eating, sat back, and took a deep breath. "Look, I know you and Bat Masterson have got big reps, and I know I ain't much of a sheriff, but I really am trying to do my job here. I got to hold the boy until either a judge or a federal marshal says different. Besides, if I let him out there's no telling what some of these folks in town will do."

"Have any of them got enough guts to do something?"

"I don't know, to tell you the truth," Birch said. "But if I let that feller out and they go after him, somebody's gonna get hurt. Don't you think it makes more sense to keep him where he is?"

Clint stared at the man, then stood up.

"You might have a point there, Sheriff. I'll be at your office nice and early tomorrow."

"I'll have a couple of men and a buckboard waiting."

"Enjoy your dinner, Sheriff."

Clint left the cafe, thinking that maybe the sheriff wasn't as big an idiot as Bat Masterson thought.

TWENTY-EIGHT

For a long time now, darkness was the only friend the killer had.

When he was a child, he'd only felt comfortable at night, because then it was easier to hide. Now he used the night to hide, but for different reasons. Fear was not something he felt now; it was something he craved to make others feel.

There was a man in jail, he knew, for the killing he had committed. To kill again while that man was still in a cell would be to tell everyone that that man was innocent and that he, the killer, was still free.

And then they would fear him.

They would also search for him, but a couple of men were already doing that, so what difference did it make?

Had they found Georgie's body yet? That didn't make a difference either. It was not a similar killing. Some people would simply feel that the poor unfortunate had simply walked off that cliff on his own.

And Georgie was an unfortunate. It had been his misfortune to make the killer's acquaintance. Of course, he had been useful for a while, but it was inevitable that he would eventually kill Georgie. He would have to, before he could really start again.

He shrank back into the comforting darkness of the doorway and felt it close around him, warming him. This was what it must have felt like in his mother's womb, he thought—probably the only time he'd ever missed his mother, for no sooner was he born than she started blaming him for all her misfortunes.

Now he was to blame for the misfortunes of others, but it was by design.

Women.

Women feared him, wherever he went. Once he'd struck, and then again, women feared him.

It gave him a feeling of power.

A feeling he often tried to avoid. He had changed towns and cities many times in an attempt to start over again. Placerville, Oregon, was just another attempt, and another failure.

Now it was time to let everyone know that he was here.

Now it was time for the women of Placerville, and their men, to feel fear.

Now he was truly alive!

Unlike his victims.

TWENTY-NINE

That night Clint watched Cory dance.

When he returned to the grounds he noticed a crowd outside her tent, and he heard the music. The bulk of the crowd was made up of men, but there were some women watching as well.

He elbowed his way to the front so he could see very clearly.

She was wearing a wig that made her look as if her hair were as dark as night. Her skin was white, in startling contrast to the hair, but no one seemed to mind. Already her body was covered with a light sheen of perspiration, causing the globes of her breasts to gleam in the moonlight.

Clint watched in awe, all other thoughts thrust from his mind. At first he was interested in the curves and hollows of her body, but quickly her pure talent for dancing caught his eye, and he watched the moves and undulations with real respect and admiration. She knew how to dance, and she knew how to play to an audience. She danced right up to some of the men, a few of whom boldly tucked folded bills into the band of her silk briefs.

As she danced she discarded scarves, often tossing them into the crowd, where men leaped for them like women fighting for a wedding bouquet.

Finally she reached the point in her dance when it seemed that only one scarf stood between her and total nakedness. She danced and teased, and then she quickly stepped into the entrance of her tent as the last scarf came off. Only her arm showed at the end, holding the last scarf, and when she dropped it even that much of her disappeared.

There was a stunned silence for a few moments, and then the crowd began to applaud, Clint leading them.

"That's the last show for tonight, folks," Pop Hingle said then, moving into the spot where, moments before, Cory had been dancing. "We'll see you here tomorrow. Have a good night."

The crowd began to break up, and Clint stepped forward and stood next to Pop.

"She's wonderful," he said.

"Yes, she is," Pop said. "She learned from her mother, but her mother never had the kind of beauty and talent that Cory has. I've been trying to get her to darken her skin so she'll really look the part, but she resists."

Clint recalled how her skin shone in the moonlight, and even how it had seemed to glow in her tent last night, when they were together on her bed of pillows.

"Maybe she knows best," Clint said. "These people loved her."

"I guess you're right," Pop said. "I never could get that girl to do anything she didn't want to do. You ready for some food?"

"Sure," Clint said. "But what about Cory?"

"She'll want a bath after dancing," Pop said. "Don't worry, she'll join us. I think Bat's already over there, digging in."

"Well, let's go and join him then."

On the way Clint told Pop exactly what they had found that day. By the time they'd reached what Clint assumed was a mess tent, he was ready to tell the rest to both Pop and Bat, who listened intently as he related his conversation with Sheriff Birch.

"Well," Bat said, "maybe he's got more sand than I gave him credit for, but I still don't think he's all that smart."

"Maybe not, but he's right about one thing," Clint said. "Maybe jail is the safest place for Lenny to be right now."

"How do you figure that?" Pop asked.

"Two reasons," Clint said. "One, nobody'll be tempted to take justice into their own hands. If that happened, Lenny would be forced to defend himself—"

"Or we'd be forced to do it for him," Bat interrupted.

"That's right," Clint said, "and either way someone would end up getting hurt."

"What's the second reason?" Pop asked.

Clint had only thought about this moments before. He looked at both Bat and Pop and said, "If the killer hits again, Lenny'll be in the clear, because he's already in jail."

"Do you think the killer will strike again?" Pop asked.

"I've seen killers like this before," Clint said, "and they rarely stop after one victim."

"What kind of a man kills a woman?" Pop asked.

"A crazy man, Pop," Clint said. "Women ought to be treasured, not killed."

Pop gave Clint a strange look, as if he hadn't heard a man voice that opinion before. He looked at Bat then, who shrugged.

"My friend has always had a very high opinion of women, Pop," Bat said. "They sense that about him, and that's why they all like him."

"I see."

"Like Cory," Bat said, giving Clint a sly, sideways look.

"I see," Pop said again.

"I thought we were going to eat," Clint said, looking away from Pop and giving Bat a dirty look.

THIRTY

The killer waited until everyone else had left. When the lights inside the place were doused, he moved out of the safety of the shadows and crossed the street. He could hear music, voices, and laughter coming from the saloon, but every other place in town was closed. This area in particular was now totally deserted.

He moved around behind the building, where he would wait a little longer—until she was asleep.

Cory arrived, smelling fresh from her bath, and sat down next to Clint while they ate. With the smell of her in his nostrils and the feel of her body close by—also, the memories of lying with her on the pillows and of watching her dance—it was very difficult for Clint to think of anything else.

"You look very different in the black wig," he said. They were seated on one side of the fire, while Bat and Pop Hingle were on the other side.

"Different?" she asked, bumping his shoulder with hers. "Or better?"

"Just . . . different," he said after a moment. "I can't imagine how you could ever look better."

Her hair was worn behind her head in a long ponytail, the ends of which were still damp.

"Do you think the sheriff will let Lenny out tomorrow?" she asked.

She hadn't been there when they'd discussed it earlier, so he went over it again for her.

"Somehow that doesn't sound fair," she said. "But I guess if he's safe . . ."

"He's safer where he is than he would be anywhere else," Clint said. "At least for now."

"It's grisly," she said.

"What is?"

"We can sit here and hope no one else gets killed," she said. "In which case Lenny will probably always be blamed. Or we can hope another woman is killed, in which case he'll be cleared."

"Well," Clint said, "maybe we can clear him before there's another murder."

She looked at Clint and said, "You don't really think that's going to happen, do you?"

He turned his head, looked at her, and said, "No."

If the dead man was Georgie, it didn't seem likely that they'd find the real killer in time.

It was time.

The killer tried the back door and found it locked. It wasn't a strong door, though, and he needed only to apply his beefy shoulder and a small amount of force and he was able to pop it open.

As he entered, he found himself in the kitchen. The smells of that day's cooking were still fresh in the air. He took a moment to inhale them, and then he moved through to the stairway behind the kitchen.

He looked up the stairs, imagining that he could hear her breathing. He ascended quietly. His ability to be silent was uncanny for a man his size, even to him.

As he entered her bedroom, she never awakened. He stood at the foot of her bed, staring down at her, then moved around to the right. His knee came down on her sternum at the same time his hand came down on her mouth. Her eyes popped open as she became aware of his weight on her, crushing her.

He kept his right hand over her mouth and moved his left hand to her throat. Once he tightened his grip on her throat he was able to move his hand away from her mouth. It was wide open as she attempted to suck in some air, but it wasn't possible. Not with the combination of his weight and the pressure of his hand.

She was suffocating—and he felt a surge of pleasure that made him wonder why he had ever wanted to stop.

When he was finished, he stood up and gazed down at her almost reverently. In death she had given him more pleasure than she ever could have in life.

He leaned over and kissed her forehead, as if to thank her, and then left.

Clint and Cory had gone back to her tent after eating. They had made love slowly and then had fallen asleep.

Clint awoke now, frowning. He looked around the darkened interior of the tent, wondering what had awakened him.

"Clint?"

"Yes?"

"What is it?"

"I don't know."

"What woke you?" she asked.

"The same thing that woke you, I guess."

"Oh, really?" she asked. She reached down between his legs and stroked him with a fine, feathery touch that had his penis pulsing. "An insatiable hunger?"

He reached for her, cupping one of her wondrous breasts. With his other hand he stroked her belly. He thought that when she danced men probably watched her belly more than anything else. How many of them would have given a fortune to have their hands where his were right now, rubbing the smooth, warm flesh of her belly.

She closed her hand over his penis as he pinched her nipple and slid his other hand down even farther, through the downy red growth of her pubic patch. The hair there was as red as the hair on her head, perhaps an even deeper, fiery red.

He couldn't see the freckles on her skin in the dark, but he leaned over and ran his tongue over where he knew they were, right between her breasts.

"Mmm," she murmured, then "Ohhh!" as his lips closed over a nipple. She used her tongue to flick the spongy head of his penis.

She held his head while he suckled her nipples, all the while running his fingers the length of her wet and sticky slit. He felt her shudder once, moaning and writhing, and then she slid down between his legs and used her mouth and tongue on him.

Whatever had awakened him was forgotten. He was willing to put it down to an insatiable hunger, which was now welling up inside of him.

THIRTY-ONE

"Adams!"

This time when Clint awoke he knew what it was that had awakened him. Someone was calling his name.

"Clint Adams!"

He sat up, feeling Cory stir at his side.

"What is it?" she asked.

"Someone's calling me," he said, standing up and starting to dress.

"Goddammit, Clint Adams! Where are you?"

Pulling on his pants, he said, "That sounds like the sheriff."

"What could he want?" she asked, standing up. She started to dress along with him.

"I guess I'll have to go out and see."

"Wait for me," she said, but he was already moving toward the tent's exit.

He stepped outside and looked around. He saw the sheriff walking away and called out to him.

"Sheriff!"

The man turned, confused for a moment, then spotted Clint and trotted over. As near as Clint could figure, it was probably not yet nine o'clock.

"I've been looking all over for you," Birch said.

"What for?"

Now that Birch had found him, he didn't seem so anxious to speak to him. He rubbed his hand over his mouth and looked around nervously, then turned and walked away with his hands on his hips.

"What is it, Sheriff?"

He stared at the man's back for a few moments, then Birch turned and faced him. There was a haunted look on his face.

"I'm way over my head here, Adams," Birch said helplessly. "I don't know what to do."

"About what?" Clint asked. "Lenny?"

"No," Birch said, "not him."

"Birch," Clint said as Cory came out of the tent behind them, "what the hell is going on? You came looking for me, remember?"

Birch wiped his hand over his mouth again, looking past Clint at Cory. Even with her hair tousled, she was a sight no man could resist—not even Birch, whatever was bothering him.

"Birch!" Clint said.

Birch dragged his eyes away from Cory and looked at Clint again.

"There's been another one," he finally said.

"Another what?" Clint asked.

"A murder!" the sheriff said. "There's been another murder!"

"Oh, my God," Cory said.

"Who?" Clint asked.

"Louisa Gannon."

"Louisa—is that the Louisa who runs the cafe?"

"That's right."

"But . . . how?"

"The same way."

Clint gave Birch a knowing look and said, "And by the same man, right?"

Birch stared at Clint for a long moment, then flopped his hands at his sides helplessly. "How the hell do I know?"

Clint turned to Cory and asked, "Will you find Bat and tell him?"

"Of course."

"Where is the body?" he asked Birch.

"I've had it moved to the undertaker's."

"Tell Bat to meet us there," Clint told Cory. She nodded and hurried off.

"Let's go," Clint said to Birch.

"Where?"

"To your jail first," Clint said. "We're going to let an innocent man out of jail."

THIRTY-TWO

When Clint opened the door to Lenny's cell, the big farm boy stood up and said, "I knew the Lord would find a way to get me out."

"Yeah, well," Clint said, "the Lord went and let another girl get killed while you were in here. That's why you're out." He was sorry almost as soon as he said it, even before he saw the shock in Lenny's big, brown, moist Virginia farm boy cow eyes.

"Look, Lenny," he said, his tone softer, "why don't you go back to the tent, get a bath, and take a rest. Bat and I will see you in a little while."

"Bat and I have to go get my money," Lenny said.

A boy with a one-track mind.

"I'm sure you can wait awhile for that," Clint said. "After all, two women have been killed."

"Yes," Lenny said after a moment, "of course."

He walked into the sheriff's office with Lenny and watched the boy leave. The sheriff was seated behind his desk with a cup of hot coffee. He didn't seem to be drinking it; he was just sitting there with it in his hands.

"You mind?" Clint asked, plucking the cup from the man's hands.

"Huh? Oh, no, go ahead. I'll get another one."

Clint sipped the coffee and found it hot and strong, but bitter. Still, it would serve its purpose.

Birch got himself another cup and sat down at his desk with it.

"I don't know what to do, Adams."

"Well, you're doing the right thing admitting it, Birch," Clint said.

"Here's something else I shoulda said before, I guess," Birch said, looking at him. "Will you help me? I got somebody killing women, and if I don't catch him he could turn this place into a ghost town. Wouldn't take much, you know, to scare people into moving on someplace they thought was safer for their womenfolk."

"I know," Clint said. He had seen it happen himself many times. The biggest, most prosperous of towns could become a ghost town in a matter of hours.

"Will you help me?" Birch asked.

Clint shrugged. "Why not? I've already started, after all."

"That's right," Birch said, "that's right. We got to bring Georgie's body in today, don't we?"

"Yes, we do—if it's Georgie."

"Oh, it is," Birch said. "I can feel it. You think he got killed because he knew who the killer was?"

"Probably," Clint said. "Maybe the killer was using him to run errands for him."

"Then why kill him?"

"I don't know," Clint said. "Maybe they had a falling out."

Clint sipped the coffee again, then made a face and set it down. "God, you make piss-poor coffee," he said.

"I know, I know . . ." the sheriff said. The man had become almost too contrite. That would start to grate on Clint's nerves after a while.

"All right," Clint said, "let's go."

"Where?"

"The undertaker's," Clint said. "I want to see both women. Liz hasn't been buried yet, has she?"

"No," Birch said. "I think she's supposed to be buried today."

"Okay," Clint said, "I'll go over there and you get the doctor. I want him to look at both bodies again."

"And then what?"

"After you send the doctor over to the undertaker, get a couple of men to go out and pick up the body. Can you tell them where it is?"

"Yeah," Birch said. "You described it good enough."

"Then let's do it."

Clint started for the door but stopped short when Birch called out to him.

"Adams," Birch said.

"What?"

"Would you—uh, I mean, should you wear a deputy's badge?"

Clint made a face. "I don't think so. If and when we find the killer, I'll just have to make a citizen's arrest."

Birch nodded, as if that made perfect sense to him, and they left the office together.

THIRTY-THREE

When Clint reached the undertaker's office, both Bat and Cory were already there. They were talking to the undertaker, who looked more like a baker than what he was. The man was huge—at least three hundred and fifty pounds—with a beard that hid most of his face.

"This is Rafe Long, the undertaker," Bat said, making the introduction.

"Clint Adams," Clint said.

"I know who you are," Rafe Long said, his beady eyes twinkling. "You're famous—you *and* Bat. I tell you, it would be my pleasure to bury either one of you fellers— uh, that is, I mean—"

"We know what you mean, Rafe," Bat said. He looked at Clint and asked, "What's going on? Cory told me another girl was killed."

"The woman who runs the cafe."

"That's a damned shame," Bat said. "What about Lenny?"

"Birch has let him go. I sent him back to the tent. He, uh, still wants his money."

"There's a boy who makes up his mind and sticks to it," Bat said dryly.

"What can I do for you fellers?" Long asked.

"When the doctor gets here, we want to look at the bodies of the two women."

"I was supposed to bury Liz today."

"You still might, but not until after we have a look at them."

"Can't blame you for that," Long said, his eyes twinkling again. "Two of the prettiest bodies I ever had in here—uh, excuse me, ma'am."

Cory glared at the man. "You're a disgusting man!"

"Yes, ma'am," Long said. "Reckon there ain't much I can do about that now." He made no apology.

After a few minutes another man arrived, and Long introduced them to Cyrus Dunne, the town doctor. Dunne looked the way an undertaker should look, not a doctor. He was tall, cadaverously thin, with sunken cheeks and thinning hair. He was in his late fifties.

"Sheriff told me to come here and ask for you," Dunne said to Clint. "Said you'd tell me what to do."

"I want to look at the two dead women, Doc."

"What for?"

"I just want to make sure they were killed the same way."

"Well, let's have a look then."

Clint looked at Cory and said, "Stay here and wait."

"You don't have to tell me twice."

"This way," Rafe Long said, and he led the three men into the back.

Louisa, the most recent victim, was laid out on a table in the center of the room. It broke Clint's heart to see her that way. He remembered her warm and alive, making love with such abandon, as if she knew it would be her last time. It also disgusted him to think of Rafe Long running his fat hands over her body, violating her who knew how.

"Doc," Clint said.

While the doctor was examining the body, Clint had noticed the bruises on the neck and on the sternum.

"What caused that, Doc?" he asked, pointing to the sternum.

"A knee, most likely," Dunne said. "The other woman had the same bruises."

Dunne straightened up and looked at Clint.

"I don't have to examine Liz again to tell you that the same man killed the two of them. Same bruises on the neck and the same knee bruise to the sternum. He holds them down with his weight, placing his knee here"—he touched her sternum—"and then he strangles them."

"Did he have sex with either of them?"

"Liz had sex before she died," the doc said.

"That was me," Bat said.

"The killer could have also—I wouldn't be able to tell the difference—but this woman was not violated in that manner."

"All right, Doc," Clint said. "Thanks."

"It's my job," Dunne said. He looked down at the body again and said, "Damned shame. Rafe, you old ghoul, you keep your hands to yourself except where business demands, you hear?"

"I hear you, Doc."

Bat and Doc Dunne walked back out front. Clint took a moment to linger behind.

"Rafe?"

"Yes, sir, Mr. Adams?"

"What the doc said goes double for me. Only if I find out you did touch either of these women, I'll come back here. Do you understand?"

"Uh, sure, Mr. Adams, I understand," the undertaker stammered.

When Clint got outside, Sheriff Birch was there with Cory, but they weren't talking. Dunne had tipped his hat to Cory, nodded to Birch, and kept on going. Bat had stopped to talk to the other two, and Clint joined them.

Clint explained that both women had been killed by the same man.

"That's great," Birch said. "And when's he going to kill again?"

"There's no way for us to know that," Clint said. "We're just going to have to do our damnedest to catch him before he does."

And that, Clint thought to himself, is going to be a damned sight easier said than done.

THIRTY-FOUR

There wasn't much else to be done until the sheriff's two men came back with the body.

Cory went back to the fairgrounds to help her uncle get the day started.

Clint and Bat found a couple of straight-back chairs and set them up in front of the sheriff's office.

"You make your rounds, Sheriff," Bat said. "Make sure the rest of the townspeople are safe this morning. We'll wait for your boys to get back with the body."

Birch frowned, but he went off to perform his rounds. He had to do them all alone, because his only two deputies were out collecting Georgie—if the body was Georgie's.

"What if we have the good sheriff deputize every able-bodied man in town and we start searching for this killer?" Bat suggested. "He's got to be holed up somewhere in the area."

"And when they find him they'll kill him."

"So?"

"Come on, Bat."

"All right, so we have him deputize three or four more men and one of us is with them at all times. How's that strike you?"

"Tiresome."

"What's your best suggestion?"

"My best suggestion would be that we all leave town, but my conscience won't let me do that. So let's go on to my second-best suggestion."

"Which is?"

"Let's look at the two women he's killed so far," Clint said. "Both young, both attractive."

"Not so young," Bat said, "but I see your point. What do we do about it?"

"We can try to predict which women he'll go after next and then have the sheriff deputize some men. One man will cover one woman at all times. Maybe we'll catch him making his next move."

"Sounds like a long shot to me."

"You got a better idea?"

"No," Bat admitted readily.

"Then let's go with this one."

"We'll need the help of someone who knows the women in this town," Bat said.

"Like you?"

"Well," Bat said, "I do know many of the young, attractive women in town, but not all of them."

"You got somebody in mind?"

"Yes," Bat said. "I haven't played much poker since I started this wrestling thing, but I have had a few games since I arrived. There's a gambler of sorts who lives in town; his name's Derek Pitt."

"Derek?"

"Yeah," Bat said. "Fancies himself a ladies' man."

"All right then, you talk to Pitt, since you apparently have so much in common."

"And you?"

"I'll talk to the sheriff about deputizing a bunch of men.

I just hope there are enough competent men in town for the job."

"We could ask Pop Hingle for some of his men, but he's got a show to run."

"Agreed: We'll leave Pop out of it."

"Although he'd be the first to offer his help," Bat pointed out.

"We'll keep him in reserve if we need him then," Clint said.

He was about to say more when they both saw the buckboard coming down the main street.

"Looks like they're here," Bat said unnecessarily. They could see something wrapped up on the bed of the buckboard and knew that the deputies had gotten what they'd gone out to recover.

They stood up and waited for the buckboard to stop in front of them. One of the deputies hopped down and the other stayed seated.

"It's Georgie, all right," said the one on the ground. "Busted up pretty bad, too."

"All right," Clint said. "That's all we needed to know. Take him on over to the undertaker—and see if you can find the sheriff while you're at it. Tell him I want to talk to him."

"Yes, sir," the deputy said. Both deputies knew who Bat and Clint were and were content to let them call the shots. The one climbed back aboard the buckboard and they both started off up the street again.

"I'll wait here for the sheriff," Clint said.

"I'll talk to Pitt," Bat said. "I might have to play a few hands with him, just to soften him up." He was rubbing his palms together.

"I know you'll do what you have to do, Bat," Clint said. "I have confidence in you."

"Well, thanks," Bat said. "I'll see you back here in a while."

Bat started across the street to the saloon, while Clint settled back into a chair to await the arrival of the sheriff.

THIRTY-FIVE

When the sheriff returned, Clint went into the office with him and outlined his plan.

"If this were a bigger town," he finished, "it might not work, but we should be able to narrow down his potential targets."

Not much of a ladies' man himself, the sheriff wasn't sure he could comment on that.

"How many good men can you put your hands on to deputize?"

"Good men?"

"Men you can trust."

"Well, the two deputies I have, and maybe one or two others."

"Counting you, me, and Bat, that would give us seven men." If they came up with more than seven potential targets they'd have to ask Pop Hingle for some men.

"I still don't know how you plan to pick out who he might go after," Birch said, feeling some confusion. "Only pretty women?"

"Not necessarily pretty," Clint said, "but attractive women, and women who live alone. If he sticks to the age group, it would be women between thirty and forty-five or thereabouts."

Saying it out loud, Clint suddenly had a feeling they wouldn't have any trouble coming up with enough men to cover their potential targets. How many women fitting that description could be in a town like Placerville?

Clint was back in the chair in front of the sheriff's office, waiting for Bat to return. While sitting there he watched the women who were walking by, and he didn't see one who fit the bill. He tried to remember the other women who worked in the saloon and figured that they would have to cover them, just to be on the safe side.

He was contemplating his boots for a moment, and when he looked up he saw Bat approaching. He waited for his friend to sit in the other chair.

"How'd you do?"

"I won about five hundred," Bat said. "Two-handed poker is hard work."

"I meant—"

"I know what you meant," Bat said. "Between Pitt and me we came up with six possibilities."

"Two of them the other two saloon girls?"

"Yeah."

"Who are the other four?"

"The mayor has a daughter."

"How old?"

"Early twenties."

"And she lives with him?"

"Yes."

"We can discount her then. Our man will want an easier target. Also, I think she's too young."

"Well then, that leaves out the banker's wife. She's not young, but she lives with him."

"Two left."

"There's a woman who runs a women's store—you know, hats and dresses and things. She's about forty, and Pitt called her 'handsome.' "

"What's her name?"

"Sally Beaumont."

"And the last one?"

"There's a rooming house at the south end of town, run by a woman named Matthews. She's a widow, about thirty-five, a little skinny for my tastes, but not unattractive."

"She'd have a house full of guests," Clint said dubiously.

"Not right now she doesn't," Bat said. "Pitt says he's her only guest, and she has her own room on the first floor, while the guest rooms are on the second."

"All right then," Clint said. "We'll count her. Do you think Pitt will—"

"Yes, he will," Bat said. "He says it will give him a chance to step up his efforts to get into her bed."

"Fine. We can have the sheriff's deputies cover the two saloon girls."

"The sheriff can look after Sally Beaumont."

"That's four," Clint said. "There aren't any more?"

"Not that Pitt and I could come up with. Pretty slim pickings in this town for eligible women, Clint. I noticed that as soon as I got here. Liz and that gal Louisa, they were probably the best the town had to offer."

"Unfortunately for them," Clint said, and Bat nodded his agreement.

"Might as well go inside and set this up with the sheriff," Clint said.

"I'll take a stroll around town, see if I spot anyone we might have missed. I guess we'd better start this operation tonight."

"The sooner the better," Clint said. "I want to catch this guy and move on."

"So do I," Bat said. "But what if he's already moved on?"

"I'd hate for that to happen, Bat," Clint said. "He'd just go somewhere else and do the same things all over again."

"At least he'd be out of our hair."

"Small consolation."

"True."

"Since we're free," Clint said, "maybe we should continue looking in the area for him. I'm sure there are some cabins we missed."

"I'm game," Bat said. "The alternative is some more two-handed poker, this time with you."

"That's right," Clint said. "Lenny doesn't want to wrestle anymore, does he?"

"I haven't spoken to him about it since he got out of jail, but I don't think he'll have changed his mind about that. I might as well give him his money and send him on his way."

"I hope you did well with him."

"I could have done better, I guess," Bat said. "I guess the problem is that I didn't really do all that well by him. His mother will probably never speak to me again."

"Is that a problem?"

Bat smiled at Clint and said, "You'd think so if you ever saw his mother. She had him young, and in spite of the fact that she's a farmer, she's a fine-looking woman."

"I don't expect you'll be going back that way anyway, will you?"

"Hadn't planned on it," Bat said. "The kid probably doesn't want anything more to do with me anyway. I'm going to take that walk and then go and settle up with him. See you back at Cory's tent?"

"Sure," Clint said. "See you later."

As Bat started off down the boardwalk, Clint opened the sheriff's door and stepped inside to set up their strategy.

THIRTY-SIX

That night they started their vigil, but even before they started they had to decide whether or not to tell the women involved. On the other hand, it would definitely frighten them, but on the other hand they had a right to know that they might be in danger—if they hadn't already figured that out.

The saloon girls were grateful for the bodyguards, and they even offered to let the two deputies sleep in their rooms with them. Clint told them that wouldn't be necessary and that the men would be very comfortable outside.

The sheriff stayed with Sally Beaumont that evening while she closed her shop and then positioned himself in the alley behind her store. Her rooms were directly above the store, and from his vantage point he could see the back door perfectly. Since the other two women were killed when the killer entered by the back door, there was no reason to think the man would change his mode of entry.

Derek Pitt assured the widow Matthews that he would let no harm come to her, even if he had to sit outside her door all night. He was only out there an hour when she opened her door, appeared in her nightdress, and asked him to come in and share her bed. *She* asked *him*, after he'd spent the past few weeks trying to get into her bed himself. Pitt would

151

have to remember to thank Bat for giving him this duty.

Clint and Bat had taken their horses out for a couple of hours before dark, but neither of them had found anything, except some empty cabins.

"Clint," Joshua said, approaching he and Bat as they dismounted.

"I'll get to those guns as soon as I can, Joshua," Clint said hurriedly.

"No, that ain't what I was going to say," Joshua said. "I was wondering: Couldn't I help you somehow?"

"Help me?"

"With this . . . problem. You know, the feller who killed those women. I'd like to help you catch him."

"You got a gun, Joshua?"

"Got me an over and under," Joshua said.

"All right, get it and go over behind Miss Beaumont's store and relieve the sheriff. He'll tell you what you have to do."

"I'll do 'er," Joshua said eagerly. "Thanks a lot. This means a lot to me."

"And don't scare him," Clint called after him. "He might blow your head off."

"Why'd you do that?" Bat asked.

"Strikes me that the sheriff shouldn't be tied down to one place. He's got rounds, and we might need him."

"I was thinking about making some rounds myself," Bat said.

"Me too, but we'll have to stick to the shadows. We don't want to spook our man."

"How soon do you figure he'll hit again?"

"Pretty soon," Clint said. "Most of these fellers kill because they like it. I figure that by now he's itching to go at it again."

"Well, I hope it's tonight," Bat said. "I want to get this thing done and over with."

"So do I."

The killer saw them.

They didn't think he saw them, but he did. They were not as at home with the night as he was. He laughed to himself, because he could have walked up behind any of them and killed them before they knew he was there. Notwithstanding what he had done to Georgie, he didn't kill men. He didn't like to. There was no pleasure for him in it. Not like there was with the women.

Of course, they *were* guarding all the right women. The killer had already picked out those four as potential victims, because the women he killed had to be young and attractive. The old ones gave him no pleasure at all. They had less to lose, and some of them—the very old ones—why, they were just waiting to die, and they welcomed it.

He was rather surprised that they had completely over-looked some other choices, and it was one of these alternate choices whom he was now stalking.

They would be very surprised come morning when they found this one.

Cory had finished her last dance and was bathing in her tent. She wondered what Clint was doing at that moment and when he would be coming over. She was thinking about him an awful lot when she wasn't with him. She hadn't liked a man this much in a long, long time. She wondered why that didn't scare her, and then she figured it out. Nothing would come of this relationship, except maybe a friendship. She decided that she could accept that. They'd enjoy each other while they had time together, and then they'd part as friends—friends who might some day run into each other again.

And when that time came, she'd be as sweet-smelling and ready for him as she was now.

THIRTY-SEVEN

Clint and Bat walked the length of the town back and forth and met up again in front of the sheriff's office.

"You know what I was thinking?" Bat asked.

"What?"

"What if this feller's got different taste in women than we do?"

"We're already going by his standards," Clint said.

"I guess I'm just looking for things that could go wrong."

"I've got one for you."

Bat frowned and said, "What?"

"What if he knows we're here?"

"What do you mean?"

"What if he's watching us—all of us—and laughing at us?"

Bat looked around, as if he could see the killer watching them.

"How do you figure that?"

"I figure he's probably pretty at home at night. That must be when he's killed in the past."

"He's a big man, though," Bat said. "Big men don't usually move quietly, and they can't usually blend into the shadows. . . . Can they?"

Clint shrugged and said, "Sam Warner saw him, but that may have just been bad luck. Maybe the fact that he had hurt himself wrestling Lenny made him careless."

"There's something for you," Bat said. "If the man was planning on killing women, what the hell was he doing wrestling Lenny?"

Again, Clint shrugged.

"Maybe he wasn't planning on it."

"You're the one who said he's probably done it before."

"Lots of times," Clint said. "But maybe he never *intends* to do it. Maybe he came here to get away from it and then just couldn't help himself."

"You're talking like he's *real* sick."

"So sick, in fact, that he probably doesn't even know that what he's doing is wrong."

"That's insane."

Clint looked at his friend and said, "Exactly."

The killer moved around behind the tent. There was still some movement out front, but, generally speaking, activity had ceased and people were simply on their way home. He'd be content to sit here and wait until they were all gone before he moved again.

Cory patted herself dry with the towel, then tossed it away and stood naked in the center of the tent. She ran her hands over her body, satisfied that her skin was smooth and flawless. She had had words today with her uncle over Clint Adams.

"You think this fellow is going to take you away from all of this?" her uncle had asked, like a jealous suitor.

She knew what the problem was. Her uncle was *afraid* that Clint would do just that, and he didn't want to lose her. She was the closest thing to a daughter he'd ever had, and he didn't want to lose her.

"Uncle, I'm a big girl now," she'd said. "I have no illusions about Clint and me. We like each other, and after we've gone our separate ways we'll continue to like each other, but I'm not going anywhere. I don't know what makes you think I'd *want* to get away from all this."

Contrite, her uncle had said, "You deserve better."

"Hush, that's enough," she'd told him. "Go look after your customers. I'm going to take a bath."

Now she dressed, trying to decide whether to go look for Clint or just sit here and wait for him to come. She finally decided that, with a killer on the loose, the safest place for her was right here, in her own tent.

Tents didn't have back doors; the killer knew that. He ran his thumb over the blade of the knife he was holding and thought, I've got the remedy to that right here.

Clint and Bat were still tossing around theories about the killer.

"If he's that smart," Bat said, "then he won't move against these women at all."

"Right," Clint said. "He'll go after another target."

There was a moment of silence between them, and then Bat asked, "But who?"

Clint shrugged, and then it suddenly hit him.

"Jesus!" he said.

"What?"

"We totally forgot about the carnival," Clint said. "We didn't include their women!"

"That's no problem," Bat said. "There are only three women there who would qualify, and two of them are married and living with their husbands."

"That leaves only one woman, and she's not being protected," Clint said.

They exchanged glances, and then both said her name at the same time: "Cory!"

THIRTY-EIGHT

It was quiet on the grounds now, and quiet inside the tent. The killer rose up on his haunches and pressed the tip of his knife to the fabric of the tent.

The knife was so sharp that when he started cutting, the parting fabric didn't even make a sound.

Cory was getting impatient. She knew that what Clint was doing was important, but still she found herself getting impatient. She hated the thought of herself becoming that kind of a female.

Her hair was still wet, and suddenly she felt as if there was a draft hitting her from behind.

She turned, saw the huge shape approaching her, and opened her mouth to scream. . . .

Clint and Bat were running from town to the carnival grounds. All of the spectators were gone, and many of the exhibits had been closed up for the night. There was some movement here and there, but for the most part, the carnival had been put to bed.

They charged through the grounds toward Cory's tent, and Clint felt his heart pounding. If she were dead he would take the full blame. How hard would it have been to simply have included her in their theory—*his* theory? Instead, he'd concentrated on the town's women and totally forgotten about the carnival.

"What the—" Pop Hingle began as Clint and Bat went running past him.

Whatever was wrong must have been serious, judging from the looks on their faces. Pop decided to follow them.

When the other carnies saw Pop Hingle running through camp, all they could think to do was follow him, and that's what they did.

By the time Clint and Bat arrived at Cory's tent, they had a crowd of people behind them.

The killer had her down on the pillows, his knee pressed to her sternum. This was different, he thought, because she was awake from the beginning. He'd had to struggle with her, swing her around to the pillows, force her down and then mount her. Now that he had her pinned, he could take her throat in his hands and—

Suddenly the killer heard the sounds from outside.

Voices.

People.

Lots of them.

He removed his knee.

Clint stopped Bat before they burst into Cory's tent.

"What is it?" Bat asked.

"If we rush in, he may kill her."

Bat looked at the tent, then back at Clint.

"If he's even in there."

"Oh, he's there," Clint said. "I can feel him. Can't you feel him?"

"Who's there?" Pop Hingle asked. "Feel who?"

Clint and Bat looked behind them and saw all the people standing there. Among them was Lenny, and he had the same look on his face as they all had on their faces, wondering what was going on.

"Pop," Clint said, speaking softly so that the others couldn't hear him, "we think the killer is in there with Cory."

"What! We've g-got to d-do something," Pop stammered. "What can we do?"

"Listen to me carefully. Have some of your people go and get some torches," Clint said. "Have one of them go behind the tent and tell me what he sees."

"I'll go with him," Bat said.

"All right," Clint said to Bat. Then he continued to speak to Pop: "Under no circumstances is anyone to go inside the tent. Understood?"

"I understand," Pop said, "but—"

"We'll get her out, Pop," Bat said. "We promise."

Pop turned and started to shout. Clint put a hand on his arm.

"Don't shout."

Pop nodded, then moved closer to the people and gave his instructions.

When a man came up to them with a torch, Bat said, "Come with me."

Not trusting anyone else to do it, Bat took the man behind the tent with him. By the light of the torch, he saw the neat tear that had been cut into the back of the tent. He motioned for the man to follow him away, and they went back around to the front.

"He's in there, all right," Bat said to Clint. "He cut himself a back door."

"What do we do now?" Pop Hingle asked.

"Well," Clint said, "by now he knows there are people out here. I guess we'll just have to talk to him."

The killer pulled Cory to her feet but kept a hand over her mouth. Her eyes were wide with fear—fear that was giving him pleasure, even though he knew there was a mob of people outside the tent.

If they wanted him, they were going to have to come in and get him.

THIRTY-NINE

"Hello in the tent!" Clint yelled.

There was no reply.

"Maybe they're gone," Pop Hingle said. It was clear from the way his voice shook that he was frightened. "Maybe he let himself in through the back and took her away already."

"I don't think so," Clint said. "It's not his style—or hasn't been, so far."

"Speaking of style," Bat said, "do you suppose he's armed?"

"Well, he's got a knife," Clint said. "We know that. Up to now, however, he's only used his hands to kill with."

"Then we can rush him without fear of him having a gun," Bat said.

"That makes us safe," Clint said, "not Cory."

At that moment there was some commotion behind them. They turned and saw the crowd of people parting to admit the sheriff to the proceedings.

"What's going on?" Birch asked.

"I think we've got the killer inside," Clint said. "I'm glad you're here, Sheriff. There's a tear in the rear of the tent. You'd better cover it so he doesn't go out that way again."

"Who's going in after him?" Birch asked.

"I don't think you have to worry about that, Sheriff," Bat said. "It won't be you."

The sheriff swallowed and said, "It's my job."

"Sheriff, I think that right now we'll just go by whoever is better equipped, all right?" Clint said. "Why don't you cover the back."

"All right."

When the sheriff was gone, Clint called out to the killer again.

This time there was an answer: "what do you want?"

"Yeah," Bat said to Clint, "what *do* we want?"

"I want to come in and talk!" Clint called out.

"You're going to go in alone?" Pop Hingle asked.

"I have to, Pop," Clint said. "It's the only way."

"Come on in," the voice called. "Just make sure you're not armed."

Clint unbuckled his gunbelt and handed it to Bat. He was about to go into the tent when he felt a hand on his shoulder from behind. He turned and found himself looking up at Lenny Younger.

"He's very strong, Clint," Lenny said, "but he has no balance."

"Thanks, Lenny," Clint said. "I'll keep that in mind."

At that moment something else came to mind as well. It was a plan, and he quickly outlined it to Bat and Pop.

"We'll take care of it," Bat said. "Good luck."

"See you when I come out," Clint said. He called out, "I'm coming in," and then he entered the tent.

FORTY

Clint entered the tent, ready for anything. What he found was a huge man standing in the center of the tent, both arms around Cory. One arm was pressed against her, just beneath her breasts; it held a knife. The other hand was over her mouth.

"There's no need to hold your hand over her mouth any more, is there?" Clint asked.

The man seemed to think a moment, and then he removed his hand. Cory was smart enough not to speak.

Clint took a moment to study the man. He was almost as big as Lenny, built along wider lines. He had a lot of curly dark hair, a low forehead, dark eyebrows, a mashed nose, and a full-lipped mouth. He appeared to be in his early forties.

"What do we do now?" he asked Clint. His voice was surprisingly soft for a man his size.

"Why don't you let her go?" Clint asked.

"I can't," the man said. "She's next."

"Why?" Clint asked. "Because we had all the others covered?"

The man smiled. "Was that you who figured that out?"

"I was one of them."

"That was good," the killer said. "One of those four women *would* have been my next victim, if you hadn't figured it out and protected them."

"And so you decided on Cory."

"Cory? You mean this one? Yes, she was an alternate. I hadn't really intended to move on to the carnival women, just the town women."

"Did it make a difference?"

"No," the man said. "I just hadn't planned on it."

"You've done this before, haven't you? In other places?"

"A lot of other places," the killer said. "A lot of other women."

"Why? Why do you kill all these women?"

The man laughed.

"That's one for better minds than yours and mine, my friend."

"Then why don't we give one of those minds a chance to figure it out?" Clint said. "Maybe they can find a way to keep you from doing it again."

"Yes, I know they can," the man said, chuckling. "It's called hanging. I'm afraid that's not the way I see myself going out."

"There are a lot of people outside," Clint said. "The tent is surrounded. You can't get out."

"I know."

"Then there's no sense in killing here, is there?"

The man looked puzzled by such a suggestion, and he said, "But of course there is."

"Where? Where is the sense in it?"

"It's what I do, my friend," the killer said. "And she's next."

"There won't be any after her, though."

The man grinned and said, "That won't matter to her. She'll be dead."

"And so will you," Clint said. "Because if you kill her, I'll kill you."

"You don't have a gun," the killer said. "You don't have any weapon."

"I won't need one."

"Are you saying you can kill me with me holding the knife and you empty-handed?"

Of course, Clint thought. The only reason this man could have had for wrestling Lenny was that he had an ego.

"Of course I can," Clint said. "You wouldn't have a chance. After all, a kid beat you already, didn't he?"

"A kid?"

"That masked wrestler. He was just a kid. If he can beat you, I can."

The killer raised the knife. He wasn't threatening Cory with it, but it was right in front of her face, and she flinched.

"I have the knife."

"I told you," Clint said, "it wouldn't matter. I'll kill you."

"Do it, then. Go ahead."

"Not unless I have to."

The killer moved Cory from in front of him but held on to her arm.

"You'll have to," the man said. "Or I'll kill you."

"You don't kill men," Clint said, "you kill women."

"I like killing women," the man said, "but I will kill a man. Ask Georgie about that."

"You want to prove me wrong, let her leave."

"No," the killer said. "No, she's going to watch. Is she your woman?"

Clint didn't answer.

"How about it, lady?" the man asked. "Are you his woman?"

"Yes," Cory said, without hesitation.

The man looked at Clint, grinning.

"First I'll kill you with her watching, and then I'll kill her."

"Never," Clint said.

The killer had his knife in his right hand and was holding Cory with his left. Abruptly, he whipped his left arm across his body, releasing her. She went staggering across the tent and fell sprawling onto the pillows.

She was free of him!

"Now!" Clint shouted at the top of his lungs. "Cory, get out!"

The sound of fabric ripping was very loud as knives pierced and then tore through on both sides of the tent. Cory saw the opening in the tent, looked once to Clint, and then ran for it, slipping through and out.

"She's gone now," Clint said. "What will you do?"

"You cheated!" the man said, his face growing livid. "She was next, and you let her get away."

"Come on," Clint said. "Put the knife down and let's walk out."

"No," the man said. "You said you could beat me while I held the knife. Let me see you do it."

"I probably could," Clint said. "But today I don't feel like trying. Bat!"

Bat Masterson entered the tent through the front, while the sheriff moved in through the "back door" and two other armed men came in through the sides.

Bat pointed his gun at the killer and said, "Put it down."

"This is not fair," the killer said.

" 'Fair' is for sane people," Clint said, "not crazies like you. Put it down."

The man looked all around him, at the guns pointing at him, and then looked back at Clint.

"Not a chance," he said, and he lunged at Clint.

Bat fired . . .

EPILOGUE

As Clint and Bat rode out of the livery they saw Pop Hingle and Cory approaching.

It was two days since Bat had shot the killer through the head, saving Clint in the process. Since that time Bat had given Lenny his share of the money and sent him on his way home.

A federal marshal had arrived in town the day after the incident and listened to all sides. He had sent a telegram telling the circuit judge his presence was not required. He saw no reason, he'd said, to detain anyone and had moved on to his next assignment.

"Cushy job," Bat had said, and he and Clint had had a laugh about it.

As Pop and Cory came closer, Clint stepped down from his rig. His intention had been to ride over to the carnival to say goodbye, but this was just as good.

"Are you moving on?" he asked.

Pop nodded and said, "Today. Which way are you two headed?"

"South. What about you?"

"North," Pop said. "I guess we're curious about just how cold it can get."

"I'm sorry I won't see you dance with goose bumps," Clint said to Cory.

"Any time you want," she said. "Just let me know."

"I will."

She came into his arms, and they embraced. Behind her back, Clint shook hands with Pop, who then walked over to Bat and shook his hand.

Clint released Cory and climbed back aboard his rig.

"Here," Cory shouted, pulling something from behind her back. "Something to remember me by."

Clint got his hands up just in time to catch it.

"What is it?" Bat asked.

Grinning, Clint held up and showed him Cory's black wig.

Watch for

BLOOD BROTHERS

117th novel in the exciting GUNSMITH series
from Jove

Coming in September!

GILES TIPPETTE
Author of the best-selling WILSON YOUNG
SERIES, BAD NEWS, and CROSS FIRE

is back with his most exciting
Western adventure yet!

JAILBREAK

Time is running out for Justa Williams, owner of the Half-
Moon Ranch in West Texas. His brother Norris is being
held in a Mexican jail, and neither bribes nor threats can
free him.

Now, with the help of a dozen kill-crazy Mexican *banditos*,
Justa aims to blast Norris out. But the worst is yet to come:
a hundred-mile chase across the Mexican desert with fifty
federales in hot pursuit.

The odds of reaching the Texas border are a million to
nothing . . . and if the Williams brothers don't watch their
backs, the road to freedom could turn into the road to hell!

An exciting preview of
JAILBREAK by Giles Tippette
is on the following pages.

On sale now, wherever Jove Books are sold

At supper Norris, my middle brother, said, "I think we got some trouble on that five thousand acres down on the border near Laredo."

He said it serious, which is the way Norris generally says everything. I quit wrestling with the steak Buttercup, our cook, had turned into rawhide and said, "What are you talking about? How could we have trouble on land lying idle?"

He said, "I got word from town this afternoon that a telegram had come in from a friend of ours down there. He says we got some kind of squatters taking up residence on the place."

My youngest brother, Ben, put his fork down and said, incredulously, "*That* five thousand acres? Hell, it ain't nothing but rocks and cactus and sand. Why in hell would anyone want to squat on that worthless piece of nothing?"

Norris just shook his head. "I don't know. But that's what the telegram said. Came from Jack Cole. And if anyone ought to know what's going on down there it would be him."

I thought about it and it didn't make a bit of sense. I was Justa Williams, and my family, my two brothers and myself and our father, Howard, occupied a considerable ranch called the Half-Moon down along the Gulf of Mexico in Matagorda County, Texas. It was some of the best grazing land in the state and we had one of the best herds of purebred and crossbred cattle in that part of the country. In short we were pretty well-to-do.

But that didn't make us any the less ready to be stolen from, if indeed that was the case. The five thousand acres Norris had been talking about had come to us through a trade our father had made some years before. We'd never made any use of the land, mainly because, as Ben had said, it was pretty worthless and because it was a good two hundred miles from our ranch headquarters. On a few occasions we'd bought cattle in Mexico and then used the acreage to hold small groups on while we made up a herd. But other than that, it lay mainly forgotten.

I frowned. "Norris, this doesn't make a damn bit of sense. Right after supper send a man into Blessing with a return wire for Jack asking him if he's certain. What the hell kind of squatting could anybody be doing on that land?"

Ben said, "Maybe they're raisin' watermelons." He laughed.

I said, "They could raise melons, but there damn sure wouldn't be no water in them."

Norris said, "Well, it bears looking into." He got up, throwing his napkin on the table. "I'll go write out that telegram."

I watched him go, dressed, as always, in his town clothes. Norris was the businessman in the family. He'd been sent down to the University at Austin and had got considerable learning about the ins and outs of banking and land deals and all the other parts of our business that didn't directly involve the ranch. At the age of twenty-nine I'd been the boss of the operation a good deal longer than I cared to think about. It had been thrust upon me by our father when I wasn't much more than twenty. He'd said he'd wanted me to take over while he was still strong enough to help me out of my mistakes and I reckoned that was partly true. But it had just seemed that after our mother had died the life had sort of gone out of him. He'd been one of the earliest settlers, taking up the land not long after Texas had become a republic in 1845. I figured all the years of fighting Indians and then Yankees and scalawags and carpetbaggers and cattle thieves had taken their toll on him. Then a few years back he'd been nicked in the lungs by a bullet that should never have been allowed to head his way and it had thrown an extra strain on his heart. He was pushing seventy and he still had plenty of head on his shoulders, but mostly all he did now was sit around in his rocking chair and stare out over the cattle and land business he'd built. Not to say that I didn't go to him for advice when the occasion demanded. I did, and mostly I took it.

Buttercup came in just then and sat down at the end of the table with a cup of coffee. He was near as old as Dad and almost completely worthless. But he'd been one of the first hands that Dad had hired and he'd been kept on even after he couldn't sit a horse anymore. The problem was he'd elected himself cook, and that was the sorriest day our family had ever seen. There were two Mexican women hired to cook for the twelve riders we kept full time, but Buttercup insisted on cooking for the family.

Mainly, I think, because he thought he was one of the family. A notion we could never completely dissuade him from.

So he sat there, about two days of stubble on his face, looking as scrawny as a pecked-out rooster, sweat running down his face, his apron a mess. He said, wiping his forearm across his forehead, "Boy, it shore be hot in there. You boys shore better be glad you ain't got no business takes you in that kitchen."

Ben said, in a loud mutter, "I wish you didn't either."

Ben, at twenty-five, was easily the best man with a horse or a gun that I had ever seen. His only drawback was that he was hotheaded and he tended to act first and think later. That ain't a real good combination for someone that could go on the prod as fast as Ben. When I had argued with Dad about taking over as boss, suggesting instead that Norris, with his education, was a much better choice, Dad had simply said, "Yes, in some ways. But he can't handle Ben. You can. You can handle Norris, too. But none of them can handle you."

Well, that hadn't been exactly true. If Dad had wished it I would have taken orders from Norris even though he was two years younger than me. But the logic in Dad's line of thinking had been that the Half-Moon and our cattle business was the lodestone of all our businesses and only I could run that. He had been right. In the past I'd imported purebred Whiteface and Hereford cattle from up North, bred them to our native Longhorns, and produced cattle that would bring twice as much at market as the horse-killing, all-bone, all-wild Longhorns. My neighbors had laughed at me at first, claiming those square little purebreds would never make it in our Texas heat. But they'd been wrong and, one by one, they'd followed the example of the Half-Moon.

Buttercup was setting up to take off on another one of his long-winded harangues about how it had been in the "old days" so I quickly got up, excusing myself, and went into the big office we used for sitting around in as well as a place of business. Norris was at the desk composing his telegram so I poured myself out a whiskey and sat down. I didn't want to hear about any trouble over some worthless five thousand acres of borderland. In fact I didn't want to hear about any troubles of any kind. I was just two weeks short of getting married, married to a lady I'd been courting off and on for five years, and I was mighty anxious that nothing come up to interfere with our plans. Her name was Nora Parker and her daddy owned and run the general mercantile in our nearest town, Blessing. I'd almost lost her once before to a Kansas City drummer. She'd finally gotten tired of waiting on me, waiting until the ranch didn't occupy all my time, and almost run off with a smooth-talking Kansas City drummer that called on her daddy in the harness trade. But she'd come to her senses in time and got off the train in Texarkana and returned home.

But even then it had been a close thing. I, along with my men and brothers and help from some of our neighbors, had been involved with stopping a huge herd of illegal cattle being driven up from Mexico from crossing our range and infecting our cattle with tick fever, which could have wiped us all out. I tell you it had been a bloody business. We'd lost four good men and had to kill at least a half dozen on the other side. Fact of the business was, I'd come about as close as I ever had to getting killed myself, and that was going some for the sort of rough-and-tumble life I'd led.

Nora had almost quit me over it, saying she just couldn't take the uncertainty. But in the end, she'd stuck by me. That had been the year before, 1896, and I'd convinced her that civilized law was coming to the country, but until it did, we that had been there before might have to take things into our own hands from time to time.

She'd seen that and had understood. I loved her and she loved me and that was enough to overcome any of the troubles we were still likely to encounter from day to day.

So I was giving Norris a pretty sour look as he finished his telegram and sent for a hired hand to ride it into Blessing, seven miles away. I said, "Norris, let's don't make a big fuss about this. That land ain't even crossed my mind in at least a couple of years. Likely we got a few Mexican families squatting down there and trying to scratch out a few acres of corn."

Norris gave me his businessman's look. He said, "It's our land, Justa. And if we allow anyone to squat on it for long enough or put up a fence they can lay claim. That's the law. My job is to see that we protect what we have, not give it away."

I sipped at my whiskey and studied Norris. In his town clothes he didn't look very impressive. He'd inherited more from our mother than from Dad so he was not as wide-shouldered and slim-hipped as Ben and me. But I knew him to be a good, strong, dependable man in any kind of fight. Of course he wasn't that good with a gun, but then Ben and I weren't all that good with books like he was. But I said, just to jolly him a bit, "Norris, I do believe you are running to suet. I may have to put you out with Ben working the horse herd and work a little of that fat off you."

Naturally it got his goat. Norris had always envied Ben and me a little. I was just over six foot and weighed right around a hundred and ninety. I had inherited my daddy's big hands and big shoulders. Ben was almost a copy of me except he was about a size smaller. Norris said, "I weigh the same as I have for the last five years. If it's any of your business."

I said, as if I was being serious, "Must be them sack suits you wear. What they do, pad them around the middle?"

He said, "Why don't you just go to hell."

After he'd stomped out of the room I got the bottle of whiskey and an extra glass and went down to Dad's room. It had been one of his bad days and held taken to bed right after lunch. Strictly speaking he wasn't supposed to have no whiskey, but I watered him down a shot every now and then and it didn't seem to do him no harm.

He was sitting up when I came in the room. I took a

moment to fix him a little drink, using some water out of his pitcher, then handed him the glass and sat down in the easy chair by the bed. I told him what Norris had reported and asked what he thought.

He took a sip of his drink and shook his head. "Beats all I ever heard," he said. "I took that land in trade for a bad debt some fifteen, twenty years ago. I reckon I'd of been money ahead if I'd of hung on to the bad debt. That land won't even raise weeds, well as I remember, and Noah was in on the last rain that fell on the place."

We had considerable amounts of land spotted around the state as a result of this kind of trade or that. It was Norris's business to keep up with their management. I was just bringing this to Dad's attention more out of boredom and impatience for my wedding day to arrive than anything else.

I said, "Well, it's a mystery to me. How you feeling?"

He half smiled. "Old." Then he looked into his glass. "And I never liked watered whiskey. Pour me a dollop of the straight stuff in here."

I said, "Now, Howard. You know—"

He cut me off. "If I wanted somebody to argue with I'd send for Buttercup. Now do like I told you."

I did, but I felt guilty about it. He took the slug of whiskey down in one pull. Then he leaned his head back on the pillow and said, "Aaaaah. I don't give a damn what that horse doctor says, ain't nothing makes a man feel as good inside as a shot of the best."

I felt sorry for him lying there. He'd always led just the kind of life he wanted—going where he wanted, doing what he wanted, having what he set out to get. And now he was reduced to being a semi-invalid. But one thing that showed the strength that was still in him was that you *never* heard him complain. He said, "How's the cattle?"

I said, "They're doing all right, but I tell you we could do with a little of Noah's flood right now. All this heat and no rain is curing the grass off way ahead of time. If it doesn't let up we'll be feeding hay by late September, early October. And that will play hell on our supply. Could be we won't have enough to last through the winter. Norris thinks we ought to sell off five hundred head or so, but the market is doing poorly right now. I'd rather chance the weather than take a sure beating by selling off."

He sort of shrugged and closed his eyes. The whiskey was relaxing him. He said, "You're the boss."

"Yeah," I said. "Damn my luck."

I wandered out of the back of the house. Even though it was nearing seven o'clock of the evening it was still good and hot. Off in the distance, about a half a mile away, I could see the outline of the house I was building for Nora and myself. It was going to be a close thing to get it finished by our wedding day. Not having any riders to spare for the project, I'd imported a building contractor from Galveston, sixty miles away. He'd arrived with a half a dozen Mexican laborers and a few skilled masons and they'd set up a little tent city around the place. The contractor had gone back to Galveston to fetch more materials, leaving his Mexicans behind. I walked along idly, hoping he wouldn't forget that the job wasn't done. He had some of my money, but not near what he'd get when he finished the job.

Just then Ray Hays came hurrying across the back lot toward me. Ray was kind of a special case for me. The only problem with that was that he knew it and wasn't a bit above taking advantage of the situation. Once, a few years past, he'd saved my life by going against an evil man that he was working for at the time, an evil man who meant to have my life. In gratitude I'd given Ray a good job at the Half-Moon, letting him work directly under Ben, who was responsible for the horse herd. He was a good, steady man and 'a good man with a gun. He was also fair company. When he wasn't talking.

He came churning up to me, mopping his brow. He said, "Lordy, boss, it is—"

I said, "Hays, if you say it's hot I'm going to knock you down."

He gave me a look that was a mixture of astonishment and hurt. He said, "Why, whatever for?"

I said, "*Everybody* knows it's hot. Does every son of a bitch you run into have to make mention of the fact?"

His brow furrowed. "Well, I never thought of it that way. I 'spect you are right. Goin' down to look at yore house?"

I shook my head. "No. It makes me nervous to see how far they've got to go. I can't see any way it'll be ready on time."

He said, "Miss Nora ain't gonna like that."

I gave him a look. "I guess you felt forced to say that."

He looked down. "Well, maybe she won't mind."

I said, grimly, "The hell she won't. She'll think I did it a-purpose."

"Aw, she wouldn't."

"Naturally you know so much about it, Hays. Why don't you tell me a few other things about her."

"I was jest tryin' to lift yore spirits, boss."

I said, "You keep trying to life my spirits and I'll put you on the haying crew."

He looked horrified. No real cowhand wanted any work he couldn't do from the back of his horse. Haying was a hot, hard, sweaty job done either afoot or from a wagon seat. We generally brought in contract Mexican labor to handle ours. But I'd been known in the past to discipline a cowhand by giving him a few days on the hay gang. Hays said, "Boss, now I never meant nothin'. I swear. You know me, my mouth gets to runnin' sometimes. I swear I'm gonna watch it."

I smiled. Hays always made me smile. He was so easily buffaloed. He had it soft at the Half-Moon and he knew it and didn't want to take any chances on losing a good thing.

I lit up a cigarillo and watched dusk settle in over the coastal plains. It wasn't but three miles to Matagorda Bay and it was quiet enough I felt like I could almost hear the waves breaking on the shore. Somewhere in the distance a mama cow bawled for her calf. The spring crop were near about weaned by now, but there were still a few mamas that wouldn't cut the apron strings. I stood there reflecting on how peaceful things had been of late. It suited me just fine. All I wanted was to get my house finished, marry Nora, and never handle another gun so long as I lived.

The peace and quiet were short-lived. Within twenty-four hours we'd had a return telegram from Jack Cole. It said:

YOUR LAND OCCUPIED BY TEN TO TWELVE MEN STOP CAN'T BE SURE WHAT THEY'RE DOING BECAUSE THEY RUN STRANGERS OFF STOP APPEAR TO HAVE A GOOD MANY CATTLE GATHERED STOP APPEAR TO BE FENCING STOP ALL I KNOW STOP

I read the telegram twice and then I said, "Why, this is crazy as hell! That land wouldn't support fifty head of cattle."

We were all gathered in the big office. Even Dad was there, sitting in his rocking chair. I looked up at him. "What do you make of this, Howard?"

He shook his big, old head of white hair. "Beats the hell out of me, Justa. I can't figure it."

Ben said, "Well, I don't see where it has to be figured.

I'll take five men and go down there and run them off. I don't care what they're doing. They ain't got no business on our land."

I said, "Take it easy, Ben. Aside from the fact you don't need to be getting into any more fights this year I can't spare you or five men. The way this grass is drying up we've got to keep drifting those cattle."

Norris said, "No, Ben is right. We can't have such affairs going on with our property. But we'll handle it within the law. I'll simply take the train down there, hire a good lawyer, and have the matter settled by the sheriff. Shouldn't take but a few days."

Well, there wasn't much I could say to that. We couldn't very well let people take advantage of us, but I still hated to be without Norris's services even for a few days. On matters other than the ranch he was the expert, and it didn't seem like there was a day went by that some financial question didn't come up that only he could answer. I said, "Are you sure you can spare yourself for a few days?"

He thought for a moment and then nodded. "I don't see why not. I've just moved most of our available cash into short-term municipal bonds in Galveston. The market is looking all right and everything appears fine at the bank. I can't think of anything that might come up."

I said, "All right. But you just keep this in mind. You are not a gun hand. You are not a fighter. I do not want you going anywhere near those people, whoever they are. You do it legal and let the sheriff handle the eviction. Is that understood?"

He kind of swelled up, resenting the implication that he couldn't handle himself. The biggest trouble I'd had through the years when trouble had come up had been keeping Norris out of it. Why he couldn't just be content to be a wagon load of brains was more than I could understand. He said, "Didn't you just hear me say I intended to go through a lawyer and the sheriff? Didn't I just say that?"

I said, "I wanted to be sure you heard yourself."

He said, "Nothing wrong with my hearing. Nor my approach to this matter. You seem to constantly be taken with the idea that I'm always looking for a fight. I think you've got the wrong brother. I use logic."

"Yeah?" I said. "You remember when that guy kicked you in the balls when they were holding guns on us? And then we chased them twenty miles and finally caught them?"

He looked away. "That has nothing to do with this."

"Yeah?" I said, enjoying myself. "And here's this guy, shot all to hell. And what was it you insisted on doing?"

Ben laughed, but Norris wouldn't say anything.

I said, "Didn't you insist on us standing him up so you could kick him in the balls? Didn't you?"

He sort of growled, "Oh, go to hell."

I said, "I just want to know where the logic was in that."

He said, "Right is right. I was simply paying him back in kind. It was the only thing his kind could understand."

I said, "That's my point. You just don't go down there and go to paying back a bunch of rough hombres in kind. Or any other currency for that matter."

That made him look over at Dad. He said, "Dad, will you make him quit treating me like I was ten years old? He does it on purpose."

But he'd appealed to the wrong man. Dad just threw his hands in the air and said, "Don't come to me with your troubles. I'm just a boarder around here. You get your orders from Justa. You know that."

Of course he didn't like that. Norris had always been a strong hand for the right and wrong of a matter. In fact, he may have been one of the most stubborn men I'd ever met. But he didn't say anything, just gave me a look and muttered something about hoping a mess came up at the bank while he was gone and then see how much boss I was.

But he didn't mean nothing by it. Like most families, we fought amongst ourselves and, like most families, God help the outsider who tried to interfere with one of us.